IMPORTANT ARTIFACTS AND PERSONAL PROPERTY FROM
THE COLLECTION OF LENORE DOOLAN AND HAROLD MORRIS,
INCLUDING BOOKS, STREET FASHION, AND JEWELRY

IMPORTANT ARTIFACTS AND PERSONAL PROPERTY FROM THE COLLECTION OF LENORE DOOLAN AND HAROLD MORRIS, INCLUDING BOOKS, STREET FASHION, AND JEWELRY

Leanne Shapton

BLOOMSBURY

LONDON · NEW DELHI · NEW YORK · SYDNEY

First published in Great Britain 2009

Copyright © 2009 by Leanne Shapton

Lot photographs by Jason Fulford. Refrigerator series by Kristin Sjaarda. Snapshots of Doolan and Morris by Leanne Shapton and Michael Schmelling. Additional photography by Derek Shapton.

Grateful acknowledgment is made for permission to reprint lyrics from "Nobody," words and music by Paul Simon. Copyright © 1980 by Paul Simon. Used by permission of the publisher, Paul Simon Music.

The moral right of the author has been asserted

Bloomsbury Publishing, London, New Delhi, New York and Sydney

Bloomsbury Publishing Plc, 50 Bedford Square, London WC1B 3DP

A CIP catalogue record for this book is available from the British Library

ISBN 978 1 4088 0472 8
10 9 8 7 6 5

Designed by Leanne Shapton

Printed and bound in Great Britain by CPI Group (UK) Ltd, Croydon CR0 4YY

www.bloomsbury.com/leanneshapton

"That ashtray stood beside the bed. On the lady's side."

"I'll certainly treasure the memento," I said.

"If ashtrays could speak, sir."

"Indeed, yes."

—Graham Greene, *The End of the Affair*

We seek the absolute everywhere, and only ever find things.

—Novalis

IMPORTANT ARTIFACTS AND

PERSONAL PROPERTY

FROM THE COLLECTION OF

LENORE DOOLAN AND HAROLD MORRIS,

INCLUDING BOOKS, STREET FASHION,

AND JEWELRY

Strachan & Quinn Auctioneers, February 14, 2009
10 a.m. and 2 p.m. EST

We have decided to introduce this catalog with text from a postcard written in 2008 by Harold Morris, whose items are being auctioned off here, along with those of Lenore Doolan, and objects given to the couple by friends and family.

—*Strachan & Quinn, 2009*

Dear Lenore,

I'll be in town for a few days next month on assignment. It would be good to see you. I've written letters to you, but they are still here in my drawer.

Remember we ran into each other at the Oyster Bar a year ago, and walking home that night you asked: Is there a relationship you ever had that you regretted ending? I didn't say anything, but I wish I had said, Yes, you. That would be my answer.

I don't know what your situation is now. Jaclyn and I are taking a break. Alone again!

Your

Hal

1001

1002

1003

1004

LOT 1001

A photograph of Lenore Doolan, age 26

An original color print of Doolan at her desk at *The New York Times,* 2002. Taken by Adam Bainbridge, a coworker. 4 x 6 in.
$10–20

LOT 1002

A passport photograph of Harold Morris, age 39

An original print of Morris, taken in 2002 prior to a photography assignment in the Philippines. 2 x 2 in.
$10–20

LOT 1003

An invitation

An invitation to a Halloween party, October 31, 2002, given by Morris's close friends, photography agents Rekha Subramanian and Paulo Vitale. 4 x 5¼ in.
$5–10

LOT 1004

A group of photographs

Lenore Doolan and her college friend Kyle Kaplan are seen dressed up for Halloween. 6 x 4 in.
$10–20   (3)

1005

1006

LOT 1005

A photograph of Morris and Doolan

A photograph of Morris and Doolan at the Subramanian-Vitale Halloween party. Morris is dressed as Harry Houdini and Doolan as Lizzie Borden. First known photograph of the couple together. Photographer unknown. Small tack holes in corners. 4 x 6 in.

$25–30

LOT 1006

A handwritten notation

A short handwritten notation in ballpoint pen on a green cocktail napkin. Reads: *"lenore_doolan@nytimes.com."* Some wear and creasing. 5 x 5 in.

$15–20

LOT 1007

A handwritten letter

A handwritten letter from Ann Doolan to her sister Lenore, dated November 1, 2002, reading in part: *"That's crazy you'd met him before—goes to show it IS all timing. I like the sound of him. Probably what you thought was badgering was just plain old-fashioned ardor. Should we be alarmed he was Harry Houdini? Perhaps he'll always come back to you OR he's a master of escape . . ."* Pale pink G. Lalo, Vergé de France paper. 8 x 5¾ in.

Not illustrated.

$15–20

1008

1009

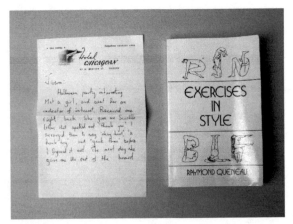

1010

LOT 1008
A colorful shirt and postcard
A brightly patterned cotton shirt with unique large sequined appliqué. Label inside collar reads "Marjan Pejoski." Some fading and wear. Size S. Included is a postcard of a Wolfgang Tillmans photograph from the Museum of Modern Art, enclosed with the original gift. Morris's short note to Doolan in ballpoint ink reads in full: *"Nobody ever buys me clothes."*
$20–30

LOT 1009
Board game pieces and board
Eight Scrabble letter pieces in a paper envelope, spelling out *"THANK YOU."* Included is an original Scrabble board game (copyright © 1987). All pieces intact, some wear to corners of board.
$20–30

LOT 1010
Queneau, Raymond
Exercises in Style (New Directions, 1981), paperback edition. Laid into page 114 is an unfinished letter from Harold Morris to his closest friend, photographer Jason Frank, on Hotel Chicagoan stationery, dated November 4, 2002. Reads in part: *"She gave me Scrabble letters that spelled out "thank you," I arranged them to say "okay hunt," "a hunk toy," and "yank thou" before I figured it out. The next day she gave me the rest of the board . . ."* 10 x 7 in.
$10–20

1012

LOT 1011

A printout of an e-mail containing directions, with a handwritten notation

An e-mail dated November 25, 2002, from Morris to Doolan giving directions to a house in Croton Falls, NY. Handwritten in ballpoint pen in Doolan's hand is a note reading in full: *"Thanksgiving / Croton Falls / Friday / Grand Central Metro-North / Sweet potatoes / Dessert . . . pumpkin cake / banana loaf / buttertarts? / Gma's recipe / Wine? / HIM / HIM / HIM / HAL."* 11 x 8½ in.
Not illustrated.
$15–20

LOT 1012

A group of Polaroids

Six Polaroids of Doolan trying on various casual outfits, taken by her friend, fashion stylist Jessica Frost.
3½ x 4 in.
$20–30

(6)

1013

1014

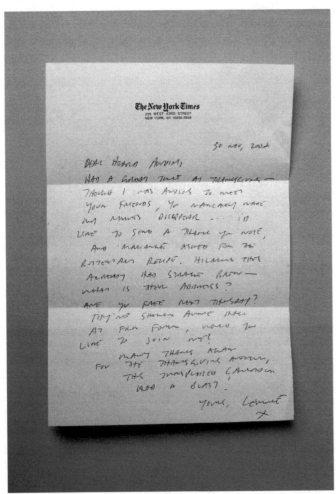

1015

LOT 1013
A DVD
A DVD of the film *Strange Brew* featuring Bob and Doug McKenzie (Dave Thomas and Rick Moranis). Good condition.
7½ x 5½ x ½ in.
$10–20

LOT 1014
A color photograph
A photograph of Doolan and Morris at Thanksgiving dinner. Photographer unknown. Small tack holes in corners. 4 x 6 in.
$10–20

Doolan is wearing an outfit seen in Lot 1012.

LOT 1015
A handwritten note
A handwritten note from Doolan to Morris on *New York Times* letterhead. Reads in part: *"Dear Harold Houdini, Had a great time at Thanksgiving—though I was anxious to meet your friends, you magically made my nerves disappear . . . I'd like to send a thank you note, and Marianne asked for the buttertart recipe. Hilarious they already had Strange Brew—What is their address?"* 10½ x 7¼ in.
$15–20

1017

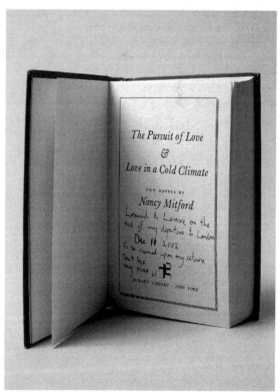

1018

LOT 1016
A pair of movie tickets
A pair of unused tickets to *Annie Hall* at the Film Forum, New York. 2½ x 1½ in.
Not illustrated.
$5–15

LOT 1017
A theater playbill for *Dinner at Eight*
A theater playbill for *Dinner at Eight* at the Vivian Beaumont Theatre. Handwriting in margins alternates between Doolan and Morris: *"Are you crying? / No, allergies. / Crying!"* 8½ x 5¾ in.
$10–15

LOT 1018
A pair of color photographs
One photograph of Doolan waiting outside Morris's apartment, at 11A Sherman Street, Brooklyn. The other of Morris waiting outside Doolan's West Village apartment at 84 Grove Street. 4 x 6 in.
$20–40   (2)

LOT 1019
Mitford, Nancy
The Pursuit of Love and *Love in a Cold Climate* (Modern Library Edition, 1982), hardcover edition. No dust jacket. Inscription reads: *"Loaned to Lenore on the eve of my departure to London, Dec 11 2002. To be claimed upon my return. Don't lose my place H."* 6 x 9 x 1¼ in.

1019

LOT 1020

A group of eleven postcards

Eleven postcards sent from Morris to Doolan over the course of Morris's three-week trip to England, December 11–30, 2002. Sizes vary.

$30–50 (11)

1. Postcard of Diana, Princess of Wales. Postmarked December 12, 2002, from London, England. Verso reads in part: *"Going I know not whither and fetching I know not what, for my gray-eyed princess. Your Irish-Catholic denial has whetted my desire. (Wait, are you Catholic?) Your gauntlet of a mere ten postcards is child's play. Your promise of surrender, my ever-fixed mark. You will certainly have all ten, fear not! This first one I write to you from the Charlotte St. Hotel, over my breakfast kippers. Thinking fearsomely fondly of you and not looking forward to these bleak weeks . . ."*

2. Postcard of the photograph "Little Red Riding Dior" by Jack Pedota, 1992. Postmarked December 13, 2002, from London, England. Verso reads in full: *"Buttertart, received your charming Polaroid this morning. Not sure about the dress. Too simple, too black, too sober for you, although you DO look very nice in it. Am wild with jealousy of every man (and some of the women) at your office party. x"* (See Lot 1021 for Doolan's Polaroid.)

3. Postcard of the Balthus painting *Sleeping Girl* (1943). Postmarked December 14, 2002, from London, England. Verso reads in part: *"Attended an opening at the Tate last night. Snuck away from the wine swilling to look at a lovely Balthus on 3rd floor. Imagined that you were beside me and we were looking at it together . . ."*

4. Postcard of a double-decker bus. Postmarked December 16, 2002, from London, England. Verso reads in full: *"Dearest Lenore: / Thank you for your letter (I love your letters!). Am sending something over the pond to you pronto, so look out for it. Will use the parental address as instructed. Here's my sked: / Dec. 19–23 Charlotte St. Hotel 15–17 Charlotte St. London W1T 1RJ / Dec. 23–28 (with Mum) Orchard House, Barkestone-Le-Vale, Notts, England WR12 7DU phone: 01386.852255 / I will call you, and of course call me anytime (I don't mind being woken!). I miss you so much, Hal."*

5. Postcard of the Man Ray photograph "Lips," c. 1930. Postmarked December 21, 2002, from London, England. Verso reads in part: *"Pissing rain here, work boring, missing you and thinking of your face all the time / all the time / all the time . . ."*

6. Postcard of the Elizabeth Salon, Belvoir Castle. Postmarked December 25, 2002, from Nottinghamshire, England. Verso reads in part: *"Thank you, oh thank you for your lovely package! I was beginning to think I'd imagined our whole affair, that I was a lunatic sending these cards off into the ether. I have put the little kangaroo on my bedside table, and immediately gobbled the buttertart. The CD has been on heavy rotation in my rented Peugeot, the lavender shirt fits perfectly, and all of the reading material is wonderful. I look forward to a closer inspection on the plane back to ~~America~~, you. / Merry Christmas darling."*

7. Postcard of *The Kiss* by Auguste Rodin. Postmarked December 28, 2002, from Worcestershire, England. Verso reads: *"Nose, hand, wrist, penis, lips, and toes. Longingly, Harold."* Drawn in ballpoint pen are the outlines of aforementioned parts.

8. Postcard of the lithograph *Elizabeth I 1966* by Gerhard Richter, postmarked December 27, 2002, from Nottinghamshire, England. Reads in full: *"They say much can be learned about a man's capacity for a loving relationship by the way he treats his mother. My mother and I are not close, but I do call her every week, and I write you this postcard on the train back from X-mas spent with her. We nibbled prawn cocktail and quaffed ginger beer at the Red Lion every night. Am dying for a Bloody Mary. Missing you my sweetest tart. Hal X. P.S. hope that last card wasn't too much, am fretting it a bit."*

9. Postcard of Anne Boleyn from the National Portrait Gallery. Postmarked December 22, 2002, from London, England. Verso reads in part : *"Two in the same day! I wonder which will arrive first . . ."*

10. Postcard of the Nan Goldin photograph "Joey and Andres in Bed, Berlin, 1992." Postmarked December 22, 2002, from London, England. Verso reads in part: *"'Love, O careless Love . . .' I hear my ill-spirit sob in each blood cell . . ."* The quote is from "Skunk Hour" by Robert Lowell, one of Morris's favorite poets.

11. Postcard of London at night. Postmarked December 29, 2002, from London, England. Reads in full: *"I fly tomorrow!! Am looking forward to our reunion—St. Regis! SWANKY! X H"*

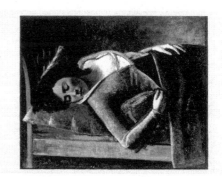

The Princess of Wales

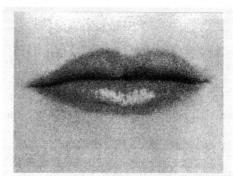

1020

1021

LOT 1021
A Polaroid photograph

A photograph of Doolan in a cocktail dress. A Post-it note affixed to the back reads: *"Had to buy a new dress this weekend for the office Christmas party!—what thinks you?"* 3½ x 4 in.

$10–20

1022

LOT 1022
A mix CD

A homemade mix CD made by Doolan for Morris titled *"Seasonal Ditty's for Hittymitty from Butterbitty."* Song list: *"Snowflake Music,"* Mark Mothersbaugh / *"Winter a Go-Go,"* Yo La Tengo / *"Fox in the Snow,"* Belle and Sebastian / *"Song for the Myla Goldberg,"* The Decemberists / *"Makin Angels,"* Destroyer / *"Maybe This Christmas,"* Ron Sexsmith / *"Let's Not and Say We Did,"* Silver Jews / *"At the First Fall of Snow,"* Hank Williams / *"Aliens (Christmas 1988),"* The Rheostatics / *"Flowers in December,"* Mazzy Star / *"Better Be Home Soon,"* Crowded House / *"Guiding Light,"* Television / *"Come in from the Cold,"* Joni Mitchell / *"Bells On,"* Sloan / *"The Fairest of the Seasons,"* Nico. 4¾ x 5½ in.

$20–35

1023

LOT 1023
A postcard

A postcard of the RCA Building, New York City, sent to Morris from Doolan. Verso reads in full: *"THAT'S TEN! See you at the St. Regis, 6 pm December 30. L."* 6 x 4 in.

$10–20

1024

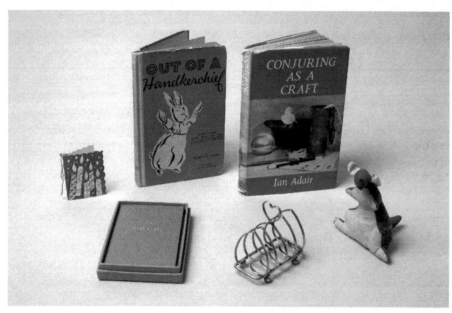

1025

LOT 1024

A group of objects

A VHS tape of *The Party* (MGM video, 1994). A paperback copy of the screenplay for *Masculine Feminine* by Jean–Luc Godard (Grove Press, 1969). A pair of antique pineapple salt and pepper shakers. A Gucci vintage silver belt. All in good condition, some wear to the book. A homemade card reading: *"A few of my favorite things . . . tho' you are nearing the top of that list! Happy Christmas, lovingly, H."*

$50–75 (5)

LOT 1025

A group of objects

A book titled *Out of a Handkerchief* by Frances E. Jacobs (Lothrop, Lee & Shepard Co., 1942). A book titled *Conjuring as a Craft* by Ian Adair (David & Charles: Newton Abbot, 1970). A small stuffed kangaroo. A sterling silver heart-shaped toast rack. A green calfskin Smythson of Bond Street "Travels and Experiences" notebook. A card reading: *"Merry XXOOXXmas, xx LD."*

$50–75 (6)

LOT 1026

An agenda

A Smythson of Bond Street Day-to-a-page Diary, 2002. The December 30 page reads in part: *"Mani/pedi, 11:30 / Tulips / Pick up prescription / Cleaners / R. Lowell / butterscotch éclairs / eggs / double cream / Blancmange due / Write Hugh? / Cancel w/Jess / coffee / soy latte / rice cake / bran muffin, Diet Coke / mince tart (2).* Facing page reads: *"Lemon bar / tea / coffee / popcorn / avocado / crabcakes / panettone."* 7½ x 5½ in.

$15–25

LOT 1027

A handwritten note and envelope

A note on St. Regis stationery, in Doolan's hand. Reads: *"Please join me in room 1045. x L."* 8¼ x 6 in.

$10–20

Included in lot is a St. Regis envelope with various inscriptions on the back reading: *"Come to room 1045"* / *"Am in room 1045"* / *"Meet me in room 1045"* / *"See you in room 1045"*

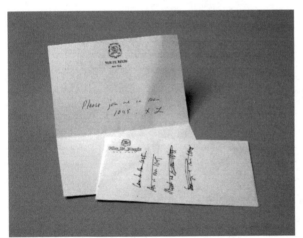

LOT 1028

A pair of men's pajamas

One pair of men's pajamas from Brooks Brothers. Royal blue. Some wear, some holes and stains. Size M.

$20–30

LOT 1029

Mousepad

Mousepad printed with a photograph of two éclairs on a plate, made by Morris for Doolan, January 2003. Some wear. 7¾ x 9 in.

Not illustrated.

$10–20

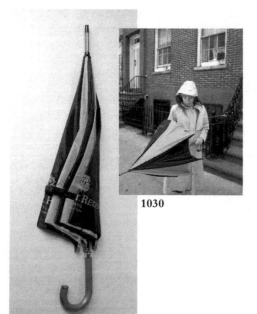

1030

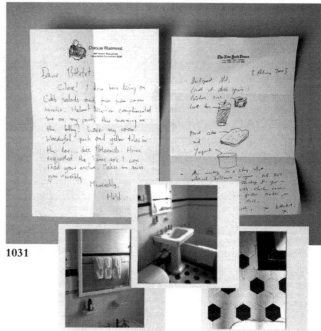

1031

LOT 1030
A St. Regis Umbrella
A brown-and-white St. Regis Hotel umbrella. Good
condition, some wear. Length 29 in.

$10–20

Included in lot is a photograph of Doolan on her street holding the
umbrella. 6 x 4 in.

LOT 1031
A pair of handwritten letters
A handwritten letter from Doolan to Morris, dated
February 5, 2003, on *New York Times* letterhead. Reads in
full, with drawings: *"Darlingest Hal, Lunch at desk again:
cafeteria sushi, iced tea, pound cake, and yogurt. Am working on
story about artisanal balsamic vinegar. nb NOT good on sushi . . .
Thinking of you in L.A. on set . . . possibly chicken caesar salad,
craft service grilled reuben, or a taco from Poquito Mas. Missing
you very much, your Buttertart."* 10½ x 7¼ in.
A handwritten letter on Château Marmont letterhead,
dated February 10, 2003. Reads in full: *"Dear Bttrtrt: Close!
I have been living on cobb salads and fries from room service.
Helmut Newton complimented me on my pants this morning in
the lobby! Love my room. Wonderful pink and yellow tiles in the
loo . . . See Polaroids. Have requested the Times so's I can read
your section. Makes me miss you terribly. Miserably, Hrld."* 8¼ x
6 in.

$10–20   (2)

Included in lot are three Polaroids of the bathroom in room 29.

LOT 1032
Fortune
A fortune-cookie fortune, kept by Morris in his wallet,
reading: *"In life, it's good not to get too comfortable."* 2¼ x ⅝ in.
Not illustrated.

$5–10

LOT 1033
A printout of an e-mail containing flight information
A printout of an e-mail exchange between Doolan and
Morris. Reads in full:
From: lenore_doolan@nytimes.com
To: hmorris256@yahoo.com
Subject: Arrivals!
*13 Feb 03 / 209 / New York, JFK 11:30am / Long Beach,
CA 2:43pm*
*16 Apr 03 / 212 / Long Beach, CA 12:55pm / New York,
JFK 9:10pm*
On Feb 11, 2003 at 2:10am hmorris256 wrote:
Great! fingers crossed, missing you. H
On Feb 10, 2003 at 3:39pm lenore_doolan wrote:
*Hal, Just got your message, will try to arrange for someone to fill
in. Will keep you posted. Visions of valentines!!*
xo Lenore
8½ x 11 in.
Not illustrated.

$10–20

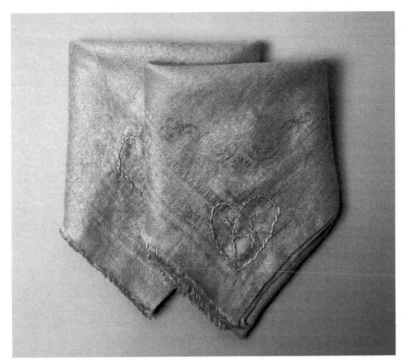

1035

LOT 1034
A handwritten list
A handwritten list on the back of a Con Edison bill envelope. Reads: *"Hoch y bring / Carr's crackers / Green dress?? / Cetaphil / Do napkins / Coffee / Orange / Kit kat / tuna sandwich / almonds."* 8¼ x 4 in.
Not illustrated.
$5–10

LOT 1035
A pair of linen napkins
A pair of vintage linen napkins embroidered by Doolan, one with the initial *L* and the other with *H* encircled in hearts. 14 x 14 in.
$50–80   (2)

1036

LOT 1036
A handwritten note
A handwritten note on Château Marmont stationery. Reads: *"Room 29 / x H."* 4 x 7½ in.
$10–20

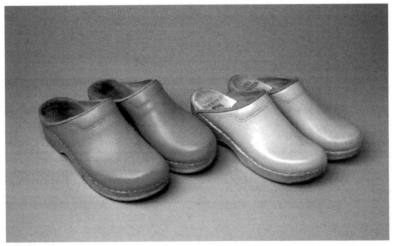

1037

LOT 1037
Two pairs of clogs
Two pairs of clogs from Sven of Sweden, 440½ La Cienega Boulevard. One pair powder blue, women's size 8, the other red, men's size 11. Some scuffing to leather.
$30–50   (2)

1038

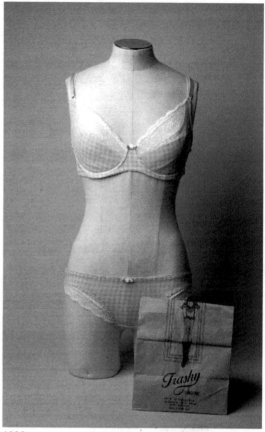

1039

1041

LOT 1038
Vintage swimming trunks
Two pairs of men's vintage swimming trunks: one 1930s, brown wool, one 1960s, red-and-pink plaid. Both good condition, some wear on wool.

$30–60 (2)

Included in lot is a photograph of Morris standing poolside in the plaid trunks.

LOT 1039
A lingerie set
A cotton bra, in pale green gingham, with matching panty, label reads "Trashy Lingerie." Size S. Original bag included in lot.

$10–20

LOT 1040
A group of six music CDs
A group of six CDs purchased at Amoeba Records, Hollywood, February 2003. Titles: Marilyn Monroe, *Anthology*; Lou Reed, *Transformer*; France Gall, *Poupée de Son*; Joni Mitchell, *Blue*; Kinks, *The Singles Collection*; Johnny Cash, *American IV: The Man Comes Around*. Some scratches and wear to cases and discs. 4¾ x 5½ in.
Not illustrated.

$40–60 (6)

LOT 1041
A candy box
A pink candy box from Charbonnel et Walker containing a homemade Valentine's Day card from Doolan to Morris. Card reads: *"Mr. Morris, my Harold, / Chez room twenty-nine, / You're rumpled and sexy / With stubble so fine / I'm here in LA / For Valentine's Day / For smooching and hooching / Will you please be mine?"* 7 x 9 in.

$35–45

1042

LOT 1042
A group of photographs
Three color photographs of the couple taken by Morris and Doolan, wearing mud face masques. 4 x 3½ in.
$20–30   (3)

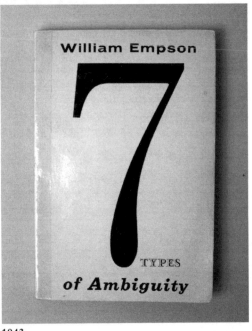

1043

LOT 1043
Empson, William
Seven Types of Ambiguity (New Directions, 1969). Paperback edition, some wear. Written in ballpoint pen on flyleaf in Morris's script is *"H. Morris"* and lyrics to the song "Bandit" by Neil Young, reading in part: *"Try to get closer but not too close / Try to get through but not be through."* 8¼ x 5½ x ½ in.
$10–20

1044

LOT 1044
A mix CD
A CD titled *Valentine Lullabies for the Lenore I Adore*. Cover is a photocopied portion of an Ed van der Elsken photograph. Song list: *Johnny Cash, "If You Could Read My Mind" / Björk, "Bachelorette" / George Harrison, "My Sweet Lord" / Bee Gees, "Hold On" / Nick Drake, "Northern Sky" / Caetano Veloso, "Love Me Tender" / Yoko Ono, "Mrs. Lennon" / John Lennon, "Oh Yoko" / Neil Young, "Bandit" / Beth Orton, "Dolphins."* 4¾ x 5½ in.
$20–30

1045

LOT 1045
Robbe-Grillet, Alain

The Voyeur (New Directions, 1966). Paperback edition, some wear. Laid in is a handwritten letter from Jason Frank to Morris, on Resort Quest Hawaii letterhead. Reads in part: *"Can't wait to meet her. Forget about Juliet!—Come on! You always do this, you start something new and then start missing your ex. It's fucked up. [Lenore] sounds great . . ."*
7¼ x 5 x ½ in.
$12–25

1046

LOT 1046
A pair of thimbles

One Ringo Starr thimble and one John Lennon thimble. Height, 1 in.
$4–10   (2)

Ringo was Doolan's favorite Beatle; John was Morris's.

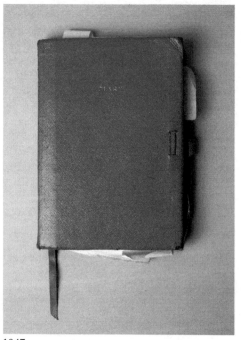

1047

LOT 1047
An agenda

A Smythson of Bond Street Day-to-a-page Diary, 2003. March 12 page reads: *"Coffee with skim / Apple / Grilled cheese / 1 rice cake / ½ slice pineapple upside-down cake / Salmon / Red wine"*
Opposite page, March 13, reads: *"Skim latte / Sushi / 2 apples / Cheeseburger / Coffee with skim / Chinese food / Apologize / Recipe for cheddar-onion tart / Story ideas: wartime baking, carrot pudding / sort-of fight over water bottle."* Taped onto the page is a fortune-cookie fortune, reading: *"Do not be overly judgmental of a loved one's intentions or actions."* 7½ x 5½ in.
$15–25

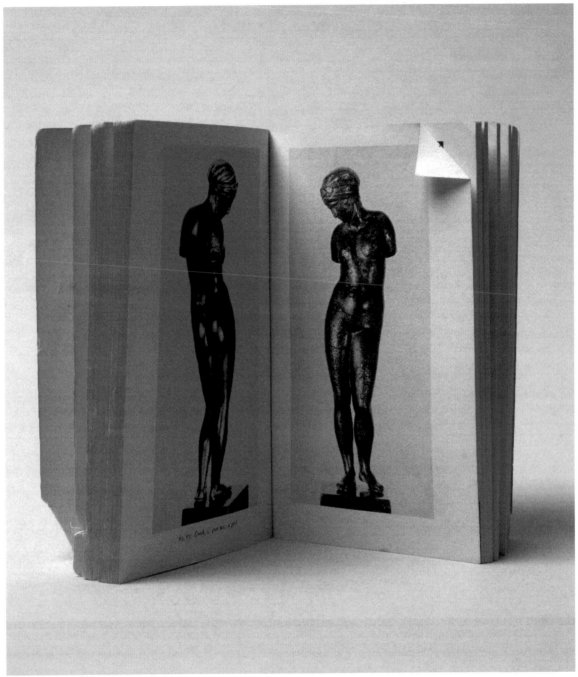

1048

LOT 1048

Clark, Kenneth

A paperback copy of *The Nude* (Doubleday Anchor Books, 1959). Jacket and spine chipped, corner of page 140 has been folded. Inscription from Morris to Doolan reads: *"Fig 63 reminds me of you."* 6¾ x 5 x 1¼ in.

$10–20

1049

LOT 1049
Sarton, May
Kinds of Love (W. W. Norton, 1970), first edition. Good condition. Some yellowing, original jacket. On title page Doolan has added the word *I*, crossed out the *s* in *Kinds*, and added the word *You*. 9 x 6¼ x 1¼ in.
$55–75

1051

1052

1053

LOT 1050

A newspaper clipping

A clipping of Doolan's first *Cakewalk* column, dated March 31, 2003, on Genoa cake. Title: "Genoese, If You Please." Column begins: *"I used to consider maraschino cherries the province of Shirley Temples and supermarket Black Forest cake . . ."*

7 x 2½ in.

Not illustrated.

$5–10

In March 2003 Doolan was promoted and made a columnist for the Dining and Wine section of *The New York Times*, writing regularly about cakes and baking in a column called *Cakewalk*.

LOT 1051

An antique cake server

A vintage silver-plated cake server engraved with the words *"Bravo Buttertart."* 9 in. in length.

$50–60

LOT 1052

A photograph and a letter

A black-and-white self-portrait photograph of Morris, aged twenty-two. Accompanying letter on Intercontinental Buenos Aires letterhead, written in black rollerball ink, reading in part: *"L, So here's one for your imagination: Portrait of the artist as a younger man . . ."* 8 x 10 in.

$25–30

LOT 1053

A photograph

A photograph of Doolan in stocks, aged nine. Post-it note affixed to back reads: *"When you were 22, I was 9. XO L."*

6 x 4 in.

$25–35

1054

LOT 1054
A series of photographs
A series of photographs, taken by Morris, of Doolan applying lipstick. 4 x 6 in.
$80–100   (6)

LOT 1055
A theater program
A program from *Life x 3* at Circle in the Square Theatre. Handwriting in margins alternating between Doolan and Morris. Reads: *"Am starving / What for / Cheeseburger / Onions and mushrooms? / Yuck / Milkshake? / Vanilla / Fries or salad? / Duh! / Leave at intermission? / Ok with you? / Yes / I love you."* 8½ x 5¾ in.
Not illustrated.
$10–15

LOT 1056
Four wooden birds
Four carved wooden birds, salvaged from a scarecrow. Written on one in ballpoint pen is *"L+H"* and on another *"H+L."* All 4 in. approx.
$25–50   (4)

LOT 1057
A grapefruit knife
A wood-handled grapefruit knife. Good condition. 6½ in. in length.
$10–20

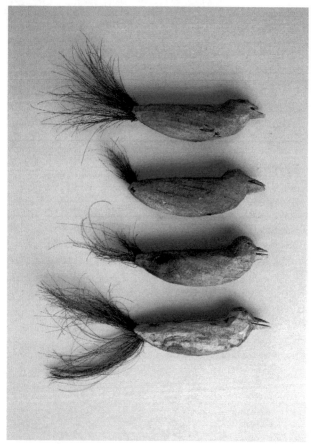

1056

1057

1058

1059

1061

LOT 1058
O'Neill, Eugene
Two paperback copies of *Long Day's Journey into Night* (Monarch Press, 1985, and Yale University Press, 1989), good condition. Some wear to pages. 8 x 5¾ x ¼ in.
$15–20   (2)
Morris and Doolan read duplicate copies of plays while Morris was away on assignment.

LOT 1059
A brooch and a photograph of a donkey
A silver donkey-head brooch accompanied by a color snapshot of Copper, a donkey Morris adopted at the Tamar Valley Donkey Park in Cornwall, England, April 2003. 6 x 4 in.
$30–40

LOT 1060
A printout of an e-mail
An e-mail from Doolan's ex-boyfriend Hugh Nash, April 31, 2003. Reads in part: *"Will be back for a few weeks, staying with my aunt Pam on the Upper West Side. Would be good to catch up . . ."* Written beneath e-mail in Doolan's hand: *"Café Loup 8pm Friday."* 8.5 x 11 in.
Not illustrated.
$15–20

LOT 1061
A pair of pajamas
Men's cotton pajamas, lavender cotton with white stripes, label reading "Coton Doux." Size L.
$20–30

LOT 1062
A handwritten note
A note on a Post-it dated May 10, 2003. Reads: *"Lenore, I'm sorry we fought last night. I will give you a call from my hotel. H x."* 3 x 3 in.
Not illustrated.
$10–20

LOT 1063

A printout of an e-mail containing address information

An e-mail exchange between Morris in Peru and Doolan in New York, dated May 11. Reads: *From: hmorris256@yahoo.com To: lenore_doolan@nytimes.com*

Date: May 13, 2003

Subject: HEY

You are a tough negotiator, but I accept your terms. These are mine: Use of stereo during aforementioned hours to play my Radiohead dirges, and tell me where you hid my black jeans.   X. P.S. There is nothing to be scared of! P.P.S. Love my new pjs but now have too many pjs. How often should one change pjs? P.P.P.S. Lima fascinating. You'd love the food! Too exotic for me though, am sticking to roast chicken. Pollo, pollo pollo . . . Marco . . . Pollo, x.

On May 12, 2003, at 8:00 PM, lenore_doolan wrote:

Am glad we spoke. I'm sorry I was so stubborn; I think I was dreading the upcoming month, and it was all coming out wrong. And upset about the rubbery soufflé. Am also not used to having someone around when I am in a foul work mood. Can I ask for a favor: tolerance of cranky moods on Sunday nights, and some weeknights between 7 and 8? If I have that I'll be better behaved. Hal, I'm so new at this, this whole relationship business, I've never felt like this before and I want things to be so good and perfect. I guess I'm a little scared. Maybe because I'm feeling really happy. Does that make sense? I can't imagine not feeling this happy feeling. So are you digging Peru?

On May 11, 2008, at 7:54 PM, hmorris256 wrote:

Bttrtrt: Thank you for calling and initiating that conversation. These things are difficult. I should have been more patient, but I know it's all good, and definitely worth it. My address for the rest of the month is Room 905, Miraflores Park Hotel, Av. Malecón de la Reserva 1035 Miraflores, Lima 18 Peru. x, Hal

11 x 8½ in.

Not illustrated.

$15–20

LOTS 1064 and 1065 removed.

LOT 1066

A dried flower

A dried yellow rose from a bouquet sent by Morris to Doolan. Kept in a Crème de la Mer moisturizer box. 3 sq. in.

$12–15

LOT 1067

A flyer for a rock show

A photocopied flyer for Les Marrons Glacés, a band playing at Elevenes, a venue in Williamsburg, Brooklyn. Verso reads: *"Thanks again for letting me crash, H xo."* 10 x 6 in.

$5–10

1066

1067

1069

LOT 1068
A newspaper clipping
A clipping of Doolan's *Cakewalk* column, dated May 14, 2003, on four o'clock cake. Title: "Cake for Tea Break's Sake." Column begins: *"The fading light, a certain restlessness, an in-between feeling—when 4 o'clock rolls around, nostalgia seeps into the kitchen and thoughts turn to what might have been . . ."*
7½ x 2½ in.
Not illustrated.
$5–10

LOT 1069
A group of striped clothing items
One vintage cashmere sweater, size 2, label reading "DBA by Theodore." One knitted skirt, no label. One knitted sailor shirt, collar has been mended, no label. One miniskirt, size 38, label reading "Sonia Rykiel Paris." One jersey dress, label reading "Cham Tex." Straps have been knotted on shoulders.
$10–20   (5)

LOT 1070
A handwritten note and photobooth pictures of Morris
A handwritten note from Morris to Doolan on a Miraflores Park Hotel card. Reads in part: *"Shoot extended two MORE weeks. Missing you, and thinking of you every time I see someone wearing stripes, or consider the cashews in my minibar and think about you eating them with ketchup. Repulsive yet charmant. Got haircut in lobby salon. Enclosed are some pics. You like?"* 9 x 4½ in.
$20–35

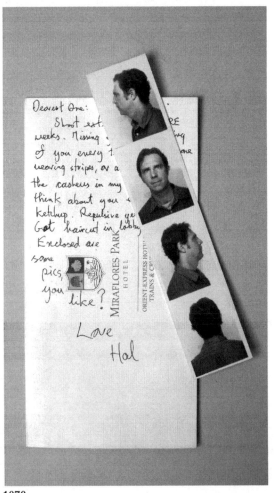

1070

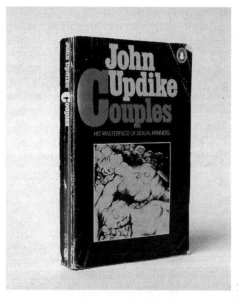

1072

1073

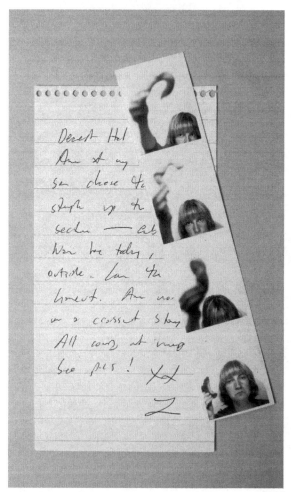

LOT 1071

A handwritten letter and photobooth pictures of Doolan

A handwritten letter from Doolan to Morris. Reads in part: *"Love the haircut. Am working on a croissant story. All coming out wrong. See pics! XX."* 7½ x 4⅛ in.

$20–35

LOT 1072

Updike, John

Couples, paperback edition (Penguin Books UK, 1977). Some wear and warping to pages, much foxing to cover. Written in ballpoint on page 79 in Morris's script are lyrics to the song "There There" by Radiohead. Reads in part: *"Just cause you feel it doesn't mean it's there / We are accidents waiting."* 7¼ x 5⅛ x 1 in.

$5–12

LOT 1073

A stack of cards in an Oscar the Grouch mug

A stack of cards spelling out *"Welcome Back Hal!"* Each letter is painted in watercolor and stored inside an Oscar the Grouch mug (chips and losses). Height 3¾ in.

$20–30

1071

1074

1075

LOT 1074
A Peruvian door hanging
A vegetable-dyed wool pom-pom door hanging. Given by
Morris to Doolan. 5 ft. x 4 ft.

$10–20

Included in lot is a photo of Doolan emerging through pom-poms in
doorway. 6 x 4 in.

LOT 1075
An umbrella
A green umbrella with leather handle. Left by Hugh Nash
at Doolan's apartment. Length 16 in. folded.

$10–20

Included in lot is a photograph of Morris crossing the street holding the
umbrella and a watermelon. 6 x 4 in.

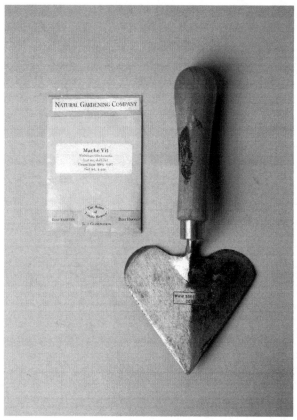

1076

1077

LOT 1076
Seed packet and a Sneeboer trowel
A seed packet for Mache Vit and a Sneeboer gardening
trowel. Some wear to handle and blade. Length 10 in.
$12–25   (2)

LOT 1077
du Maurier, Daphne
Don't Look Now and Other Stories, paperback edition (Penguin
Books, 1999). Pages well worn, some watermarks. Laid in are
two Delta Airlines boarding passes for flight from JFK to
Venice, dated June 19, 2003.
7 x 4¼ in. (book).
$5–15

LOT 1078
A pair of travel pillows
One Frette in a pale green case; one light gray inflatable neck
rest, no label. Some wear. Dimensions vary.
$10–20   (2)

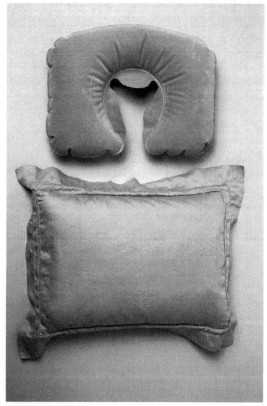

1078

1079

LOT 1079

A cosmetics case and contents

A traveling case and cosmetics. The striped Henri Bendel case contains an assortment of makeup, toiletries, and cosmetics comprising: one lipstick from Chanel, labeled "Sweet Nature"; one Clinique Neutral Fair concealer; one tube Dr. Hauschka Rose Day Cream; one tube Kiss My Face Ultra Moisturizer; one tube Dr. Hauschka lipstick in color no. 4; two bottles of nail polish, one by OPI in "Did Somebody Say Party?" and one by Essie in "The Way We Were"; one Nars blusher in Turkish Red; one tube Revlon mascara; one Revlon Colorstay liquid liner; two hair baubles; one hair elastic; fifty-four bobby pins; one tube La Roche-Posay Antihelios W Gel SPF 40; one small jar of Vaseline; two matchbooks, one from Odeon, the other from Union Square Café; one prescription bottle of Wellbutrin; one prescription bottle of Lorazepam; four OB tampons; one prescription bottle of Rhinocort Aqua nasal spray; one prescription bottle Nasonex nasal spray; one sample bottle Cromolyn eyedrops; one tube of prescription tacrolimus ointment; one bottle OXY lotion; one foil package Nuvaring vaginal ring; one small bottle of Bayer aspirin; one beaded bracelet; one Weleda sage deodorant; one small bottle Heinz ketchup; one bottle Clear Eyes eyedrops; one bottle Aveda Elixir leave-in conditioner; one nail clipper; one pair Ms. Manicure tweezers; one tube Chapstick; one packet Oral-B dental floss; one plastic toothbrush; two Lifestyles condoms; one pair earrings; one safety pin; four hair slides; one plastic tortoiseshell ring; one vintage 1960s lucite ring; one tube hydrocortisone ointment; one tube Jurlique calendula cream; one felt poppy form; one bottle of Santa Maria Novella "Eva" perfume.

$40–55

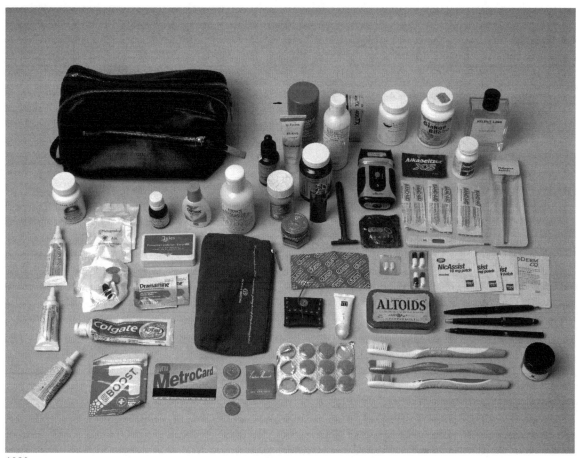

1080

LOT 1080

A man's traveling case and contents

A black case with three zippered compartments, label inside reading "Prada." Contents comprise: one small tube of Colgate Total toothpaste; three toothbrushes; one box Kodak Tri-X400 120 film; one bottle melatonin; one stick of Clinique Skin Supplies for Men deodorant; one bottle Kiehl's Aloe Vera and Oatmeal Musk Hand and Body lotion; one bottle Kiehl's Ultra Facial moisturizer; one bottle Ayurvedic Prescriptives Hyper-Acidity tablets; one bottle Jarrow Ginko Biloba capsules; one bottle Helmut Lang eau de cologne; one bottle Herb Pharm echinacea extract; one tube Nelsons burn cream; one jar Metagenics Somnolin tablets; one blue Bic lighter; one blue Gillette disposable razor; one Eltron electric shaver; one packet Alka-Seltzer; one bottle Tylenol PM; three Band-Aids; one Avanti Durex condom; two Durex condoms; one jar Tiger Balm; one bottle Pepto-Bismol; two tubes Neosporin; one tube CVS antibiotic ointment; one bottle Neals Yard Remedies euphrasia tincture; one tin Altoids; one packet Simply Sleep; two packets Tylenol PM gelcaps; three NicAssist patches; one NicoDerm CQ patch; one jar Jo Malone Apricot and Aloe eye gel; one Intercontinental ballpoint pen; one small leather envelope containing two small semi-precious stones; one Eliot Hotel ballpoint pen; one Palace Hotel San Francisco ballpoint pen; one packet Strepsils; one matchbook from the Château Marmont; one Oswald Boateng Virgin Upperclass case; 2 euros and 10 cents; one Metrocard; one packet Eboost supplement; two packets Dramamine; one box Quies earplugs; one bottle Sinex; four packets Metagenics Wellness Essentials for Men; one red toothbrush in case from Phillipine Airlines; one folded handwritten note on lined paper in Doolan's script, reading: *"Brown bikini top, in shelf on top of safe."*
$40–55

1081

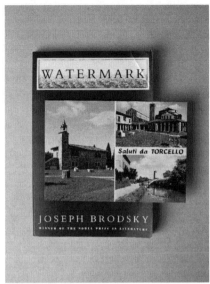

1082

LOT 1081
Three postcards of Venice
One postcard with note on verso in Doolan's script, reading: *"Ragazzo, have gone to Piazza St. Marco. Meet me in front of the red columns at 4?"* Two others with notes on verso in Morris's script: *"Some a-prezzies! You a-like? Happy Birthday! Amore, Hal"* and *"Didn't have the heart to wake you. Am in bar next door."* 4 x 6 in.

$20–45   (3)

LOT 1082
Brodsky, Joseph
Watermark, paperback edition (Farrar, Straus and Giroux, 1993). Laid into page 39 is an unsent postcard from Doolan to Kyle Kaplan, reading in part: *"Loads of nice gifts from H— Italian lessons, a sweet cookbook, and a gorgeous heavy (all beach towels should feel this heavy) Hermès towel. Am bummed to not be spending my birthday with you and Jess, but having an incredible time here. A little overcast but it's beautiful. Slightly ominous—very Visconti or Talented Mr. Ripley . . ."* 7¼ x 5¼ x ¼ in.

$5–15

LOT 1083
A towel
A rabbit-motif towel, label on edge reading "Hermès Paris." Some light wear and fading. 35 x 58 in.

$30–50

1083

1084

LOT 1084
Fisher, M.F.K.; two 45s

How to Cook a Wolf, first edition (Duell, Sloan and Pearce, 1942). Good condition, original dust jacket intact, chips and slight foxing at spine. Inscription on flyleaf reads: *"For dear Lenore, happy 27th, Venice 2003, Love your hungry Harold."* Laid in is a note in Doolan's script on Locanda Cipriani letterhead that reads: *"Café longo / bellini / cheese toast / bigoli / biblioteca / Ca' Rezzonico / Oliva Nera / Byron was a swimmer / Hal wears his sunglasses on head / Paolin / Lido."* Included in lot are two 45s kept tucked into cover of the book: Lelio Luttazzi, "El can de Trieste" and Gli Anni Felici, "Continueranno." Dimensions vary.
$200–250

LOT 1085
A notebook

Doolan's yellow reporter's notepad. Entry for June 23, 2003, reads: *"Dream last night, was looking up the name 'Ghost' in Italian phonebook, then a vampire. A woman is there, and I'm in a lineup to be killed and made a vampire myself. I am frightened and don't want it to happen. I see the man from the vaporetto, and we share a glance. Foccacia / Grissini / Piadina Romagnola / Pan di Ramerino / Ciabatta / Amaretto Zuccotto Cake / Stamps."* At bottom of list, in Morris's script, is written: *"Where does Lenore want to go for dinner tonight? Should one trust the concierge? Why does Lenore always order her salads with no dressing? How do you say 'Thousand Island' in Italian?"* 7½ x 4⅛ x ¼ in.
$20–25

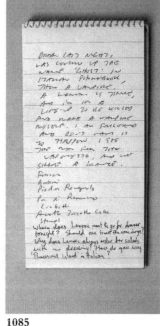

1085

1087

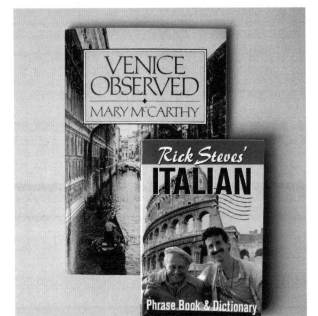

1086

LOT 1086

A group of four photographs

One photo of Doolan with hair wrapped in a hotel towel. One of the pair eating spaghetti. One of Morris on the Locanda Cipriani patio drinking a spritzer. One of the couple seated in a restaurant. 4 x 6 in.
$30–40   (4)

LOT 1087

Two signs

Two Italian dog-warning ATTENTI AL CANE signs. Purchased in Milan on return trip from Venice. 4 x 10 in.
$30–50   (2)

LOT 1088

McCarthy, Mary; Steves, Rick

Venice Observed (Harcourt Brace Janovich, 1963) and *Rick Steves' Italian* (Avalon Travel, 1999). Good condition, some wear and yellowing to pages. Doolan's handwriting on inside front cover of *Venice Observed* reads: "*Coffee / Pane / Spaghetti carbonara w/anchovies / Salad / Gelato (straciatella) / Veal thing / Polenta cake / Cakewalk due / Cried in shower / H texting, drinking, and smoking all night on the balcony.*" Dimensions vary.
$10–20   (2)

1088

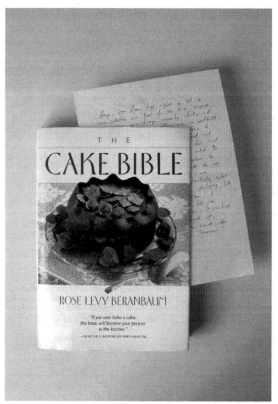

1089

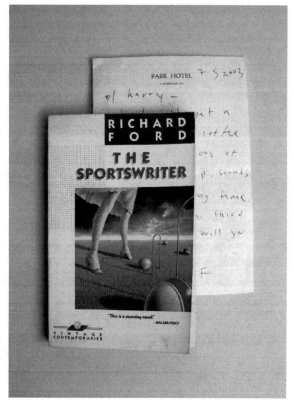

1090

LOT 1089

Levy Beranbaum, Rose

The Cake Bible, hardcover (HarperCollins, 1993). Good condition, some staining and wear. Laid into front cover is an unsent letter from Lenore Doolan to Ann Doolan, reading in part: *"Anny, was dream trip right up till we were catching our taxi to the Milan airport. The cabbie was driving insanely fast, and I was nervous because there were no seatbelts. I asked Hal to ask him in Italian to slow down, but he just laughed and said it was fine. I insisted I felt scared and he rolled his eyes. So I asked the driver in French to slow down, which he understood. Hal didn't speak to me the whole flight home, and I was just as angry. It was completely awful. Things haven't been the same. I love him so much, but it's like we don't have room for each other. It was bad. I am worried we're going to break up . . ."* Pale pink G. Lalo, Vergé de France paper. 8 x 5¾ in.
$20–35

LOT 1090

Ford, Richard

The Sportswriter, paperback edition (Vintage, 1995). Notation on inside front cover reads: *"Dial 7 confirmation 46578 / Valium (blue) / Xanax (white) / Cylexa (small white) / Kath."* Written in ballpoint pen on back flyleaf in Morris's script are lyrics to the song "Game of Pricks" by Guided by Voices, reading: *"You could never be strong / You can only be free."* Laid in is a letter from Jason Frank to Morris, on Park Hotel, Honesdale, Pennsylvania letterhead. Reads in part: *"Got your letter, sounds like Venice was an amazing time. Will be in L.A. third week of July. Will you be there?"* 7¼ x 5⅛ x ½ in.
$5–15

LOT 1091

A newspaper clipping

A clipping of Doolan's *Cakewalk* column, dated July 1, 2003, on panpepato. Title: "Bittersweet and Chewy, a Spicy Siena Cake." Column begins: *"A cake may not always be so sweet . . ."* 8½ x 2½ in.
Not illustrated.
$5–10

1092

LOT 1092

A group of six bathing suits

One black string bikini, label reading "Triumph International Soleil." One sixties mod print cutout, no label. One brown halter-neck, label reading "Eres." One pink, olive green, red, and yellow stripe, no label. One red bandeau, label reading "APC." One white fifties one-piece, label reading "Sea Queen."

$15–40   (6)

Included in lot is a picture of Doolan wearing white Sea Queen one-piece. The photograph was taken at the Orient Point rental house that Morris shared with friends Jason Frank, Toby Cwir, and Cwir's girlfriend, Alicia Diaz. 4 x 6 in.

36

1093

1094

LOT 1093
A framed photograph
A framed black-and-white photograph of Morris surfing. Photographer unknown. 8½ x 6½ in.
$15–20

LOT 1094
A group photograph
A color photograph of Morris, Cwir, Frank, Doolan, and Diaz playing Trivial Pursuit at Orient Point. 4 x 6 in.
$15–20

LOT 1095
A group of tag-sale finds
A hardcover book titled *Adventures with Hal*, by Gladys Baker Bond (Whitman, 1965). A bisque bust of Niobe. Five assorted dinner plates.
$10–30   (7)

LOT 1096
A group of maps
Maps from a road trip to Guelph, Ontario, to visit Doolan's family. Dimensions vary.
Not illustrated.
$15–25   (3)

1095

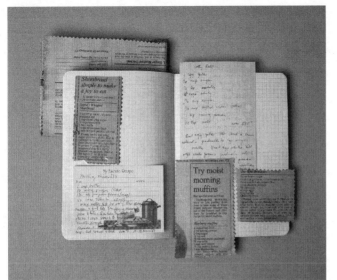

1097

LOT 1097
A book of recipes
A book of handwritten recipes, given to Doolan by her maternal grandmother, Glenda Lucas, a former restaurant reviewer for *The Toronto Star* in the 1960s. 8 x 6 in.
$40–70

1098

LOT 1098
A group of tea towels
Three vintage tea towels from the Doolan family home: one London Fog, one calorie counter motif, and one American presidents. All worn, some stains. 24 x 16 in., 20 x 14 in., and 20 x 16 in., respectively.
$10–20   (3)

1099

LOT 1099
A photograph of a blanket on a lawn
A color photograph of a crocheted blanket on the Doolan lawn, where Morris and Doolan slept outside in an attempt to escape the late August heat. 7 x 4 ft.
$20–30

1100

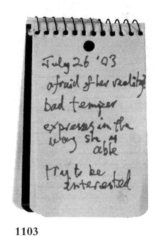

1102

1101

1103

LOT 1100

Six CDs

Six music CDs of The Fall, *Peel Sessions*. Included in lot is a note in Doolan's hand, reading: *"Sorry about the cd. I was going nuts in that traffic. Got Kyle to burn these for you! x."*

$10–15   (6)

LOT 1101

A framed photograph of Doolan and Morris

A photograph, in a silver frame, of Doolan and Morris in the back of the Doolan family sedan. Photograph taken by Tracey Doolan, Lenore's mother. 4¾ x 6¾ in.

$10–20

LOT 1102

A series of twenty-four photographs

Photographs taken by Morris of various pieces of beef jerky. 7 x 5 in.

$20–30   (24)

LOT 1103

A small spiral notebook

A small green spiral notebook kept by Morris during sessions with Dr. Jay Zaretzsky. Reads in part: *"July 26 '03: afraid of her reality? / bad temper / expresses in the way she is able / try to be interested."* 4½ x 3 in.

$12–25

1104

LOT 1104
Birthday presents, card, and note

One striped men's shirt, label reading "Steven Alan," size M. A gift certificate, unused, for Italian cooking lessons at the Culinary Institute. One Wimpy's ketchup squeezer. A paperback copy of the screenplay for *Blow-Up* by Michelangelo Antonioni (Modern Film Scripts, Simon & Schuster, 1971). Homemade birthday card from Doolan to Morris, dated September 6, 2003. Card reads: *"The catsup is for Hal of the past, the shirt is for Hal of the present, the lessons for Hal of the future. Happy 40th!"* A handwritten note in ballpoint pen on back of travel itinerary, in Morris's script, reads in part: *"Darling, Am sorry about last night, please please don't get offended about the cake, I've always loathed meringue and thought I'd mentioned it. It looked great! And please understand I needed to spend my 40th with Jase and Toby—guy thing, God knows—but was having a bit of a wobble. Thanks for your understanding . . ."*

$50–100   (5)

Included in lot is a photograph of a large pavlova, 4 x 6 in.

1105

1106

1107

1108

LOT 1105
A handwritten list
A list on yellow foolscap paper in Doolan's hand. Reads: *"Pros: Fun, good sex, different world, travel, art / Cons: Depressive—drinking? celebrity fixation, bad breath, always traveling, doesn't care about food, withholding."* Paper is folded in half five times. 14 x 8½ in.
$10–15

LOT 1106
An invitation
An invitation to a Halloween party, October 31, 2003, given by Morris's close friends Rekha Subramanian and Paulo Vitale. 5¼ x 4 in.
$5–10

LOT 1107
A photograph
A snapshot of Morris and Doolan dressed as Benjamin Braddock and Mrs. Robinson. Photographer unknown. Print has been folded. 6 x 4 in.
$20–30

LOT 1108
A photograph
A photograph taken at a farewell party for Doolan's coworker Adam Bainbridge. Photographer unknown. 4 x 6 in.
$15–20

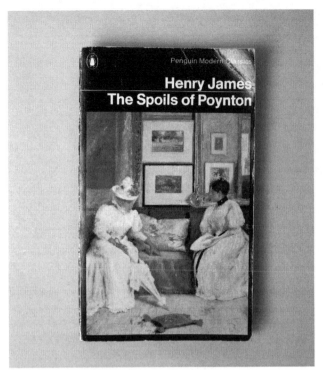

1110

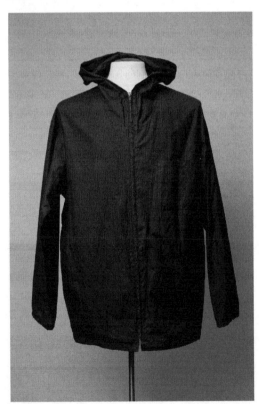

1111

LOT 1109
A newspaper clipping
A clipping of Doolan's *Cakewalk* column, dated November 5, 2003, on wartime carrot cake. Title: "Rationing Chic: Root-Sweet." Column begins: *"Cooking in the spirit of making do, of resourcefulness and thrift, is uniquely rewarding . . ."* 7 x 2½ in. *Not illustrated.*
$5–10

LOT 1110
James, Henry
The Spoils of Poynton, paperback edition (Penguin, 1971). Laid in is an unsent handwritten letter on yellow foolscap, in Doolan's script, reading in part: *"Dear Hal, My heart is so low, I turned in early tonight and brought the phone to bed as I thought you might call. You haven't called all week. ~~Hal please, after such a bad fight.~~ You used to always say 'You can call,' but lately when I do, you are either sleeping, or it sounds like I'm interrupting you, I can't talk like that. After such a bad fight, please just be there, please even if you're angry. We need to be able to talk . . ."* 10 x 8 in.
$5–10

LOT 1111
A men's windbreaker
A navy blue men's windbreaker with hood, label reading "Helmut Lang." Size M. Good condition. Laid into left pocket is a short handwritten letter from Allison Slater, Morris's former assistant, to Morris. Reads in full: *"Dear Hally, Thank you for all of your advice, and for the lovely lunch. I will find and devour those books you recommended. I've always taken to heart your advice to me, and especially now at the end of my relationship with Brian, any advice on moving forward without fear and with grace and kindness is welcome. I have always admired your spiritual outlook. God, why is love so hard? How are you and your new girlfriend? Namaste, Allison."* 7 x 9 in.
$10–20

LOT 1112

A three-piece suit

A vintage brown wool tweed three-piece suit, label inside reading "Made in Poland." Given to Morris by Doolan on Thanksgiving 2003. Laid into vest is a homemade card reading: *"Happy Anniversary Hal! Much love and endless tweed, Lenore."*

$40–60

Included is a photograph of the couple, taken by Jason Frank. Morris is wearing the suit.

LOT 1113

A pair of socks and a card

A pair of orange socks from Thomas Pink Co., Heathrow Airport. Given by Morris to Doolan on Thanksgiving 2003. Accompanied by a homemade card reading: *"Favorite moments of the year: 1. When you asked if you could try my potato salad at Wallse. / 2. Finding you at Harry's Bar after I thought I'd lost you. / 3. When you put on Nivea in bed and hum the 'Big Star' song. / 4. Jaywalking to get vodka. / 5. Seeing you in your reading glasses for the first time. / 6. Our shared indifference over the dancing cupcake. / 7. When you returned from the deli wearing my sweater and jacket after getting me Neosporin."* 4 x 5½ in.

$10–30

1113

1112

1114

1116

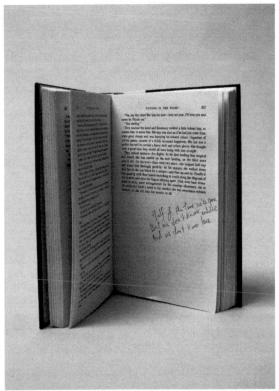

1115

LOT 1114
A color photograph
A photograph of Doolan with pie and Morris holding a cocktail, at Thanksgiving, taken by Marianne Grau. Small tape marks in corners. 4 x 6 in.
$10–20

LOT 1115
Fitzgerald, F. Scott
The Great Gatsby and *Tender Is the Night*, hardcover edition, some wear to spine (Charles Scribner's Sons, 1962). Written in ballpoint pen on page 203 in Morris's hand are lyrics to the song "Only Living Boy in New York" by Paul Simon, reading in part: *"Half of the time we're gone but we don't know where / And we don't know here."* 9 x 6¼ x 1¼ in.
$5–15

LOT 1116
A group of invitations
Four Christmas party invitations. Sizes vary. On the back of one, in Doolan's script, is written: *"Mom: yellow knit thing / Dad: scarf / Adam: Astier notebooks / Kyle: Mitts / Jess: Moro cookbook / Hal: Salad tossers? / Scarf, Skates / Coffee / ½ croissant / apple / orange / call dermatologist / flax seed? / gluten-free pizza."* On the back of another is written: *"Jared, Ian, Cam, Bryan, Chris, Owen, Geoffrey, Ted, Nico, John, ?, Peter H., Lewis, Will, Mike, Reg, Victor, Miguel, Hugh."*
$5–15   (4)

1117

1118

1119

LOT 1117
A small Christmas tree
A small Christmas tree, sprayed with fake snow. Height 13 in.
$12–20

LOT 1118
A Christmas card
A card from Doolan's parents. Addressed *"Howard & Lenore."* 7 x 4 in.
$15–25

LOT 1119
Dog salt and pepper shakers
A pair of dachsund salt and pepper shakers. Given by Morris's mother to Doolan. Unused. 3¼ in. in length.
$10–20
After Morris mentioned to his mother that Doolan was fond of dogs, Eleanor Morris began bestowing gifts of dog paraphernalia on Doolan for holidays and birthdays.

1120

LOT 1119a
Perfume bottles

Three Diptyqhe L'Ombre dans l'Eau perfume bottles, one
16 oz. and two 8 oz. All good condition.

Not illustrated.

$10–20 (3)

This perfume was worn exclusively by Doolan after Morris gave her a bottle
December 2003. Doolan collected the empty bottles.

LOT 1120
A group of gift items

A pair of men's ice hockey skates, size 11, black nylon and
plastic with white detail, back heels branded "Bauer" in
white. A man's scarf in a black-and-white-plaid wool-
cashmere blend, label reading "Maxfield." A pair of
antique salad tossers with green ceramic handles.
Dimensions vary.

$40–55 (3)

Included is a photograph of Morris wearing the scarf.

1121

LOT 1121
A group of gift items
A vintage 1968 Olivetti manual portable typewriter, in good condition. A postcard of Jesus Christ. A green-and-cream vintage cake tin, some dents, good condition. A pair of long mauve women's suede gloves, label reading "Barneys, New York." Dimensions vary.

$40–55   (4)

Included is a photograph of Doolan using the typewriter.

LOT 1122
A newspaper clipping
A clipping of Doolan's *Cakewalk* column, dated December 28, 2003, on parkin. Title: "Buried Treacle Treasure." Column begins: *"Find it impossible to let a wrapped present go unshaken? This cake might not be for you . . ."* 7 x 2½ in.
Not illustrated.
$5–10

LOT 1123
An invitation
An invitation to a black-tie dinner for a New Year's Eve party given by *The New York Times* at the Century Club. 6 x 6 in.
Not illustrated.
$5–10

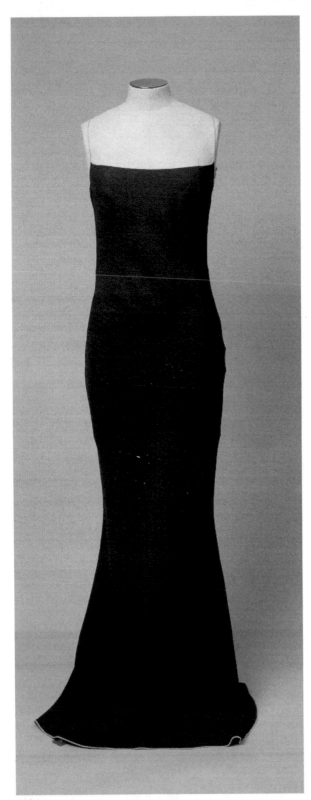

1124

1126

LOT 1124
An evening gown
A John Galliano black gown. Good condition. Shoulder straps taken up at the back. Size 36.
$200–400

LOT 1125
A printout of an e-mail
A printout of an e-mail from Morris to Doolan containing address information. Reads in full:
From: hmorris256@yahoo.com
To: lenore_doolan@nytimes.com
Date: December 28, 2003
Subject: I KNOW I KNOW I KNOW I KNOW
I know I know I know I know I know I know I know and I'm sorry!! You know I had to take this job, I need more portraits in my book—they can't all be of YOU! Address for next 2 weeks is Groucho Club, 45 Dean Street, London W1D 4QB, Tel +44(0)20 7439 4685 room 5. x's.
11 x 8½ in.
Not illustrated.
$15–20

LOT 1126
An envelope of confetti
An envelope of confetti with a date typewritten on the back: *January 1, 2004.* Mailed by Doolan to Morris at the Groucho Club. 3½ x 6 in.
$10–15

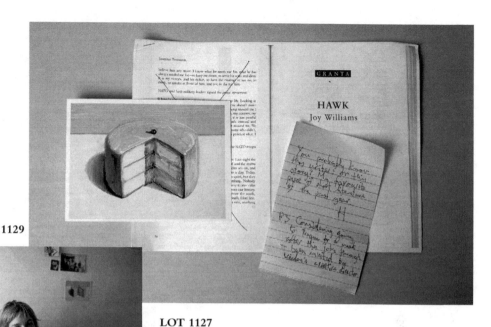

1129

LOT 1127

A newspaper clipping

A clipping of Doolan's *Cakewalk* column, dated January 11, 2004, on sand cake. Title: "Throw Me a Crumb." 8 x 2½ in. *Not illustrated.*

$5–10

LOT 1128

Three items and a postcard

A box of Yorkshire loose tea. An orange cashmere Paul Smith scarf, some wear. A sterling silver dog-collar choker, good condition, with original box. Included is a postcard of the Jacques Henri Lartigue photograph "1928 Lac d'Annecy," reading in part: *"Buttertart, You sounded so ill on the phone, am sending tea for your throat and a bright orange scarf for your neck. Also little something from Agent Provocateur . . . x."* Dimensions vary.

$40–60   (3)

LOT 1129

A postcard and a *Granta* article

A blank postcard of the Wayne Thiebaud painting *Lemon Cake, 1983*. Nine photocopied pages from *Granta* magazine of the essay "Hawk" by Joy Williams. They are stapled together with a note reading: *"You probably know this writer? Or this story? My favourite piece of short literature of the past year. H. P.S. Considering going to Prague for week after this job's through—been invited by Wieden's creative director and should probably go."* Dimensions vary.

$10–25

Included is a photograph of Doolan taken by Morris, in her West Village apartment, with postcard affixed to wall in background, 4 x 6 in.

1128

49

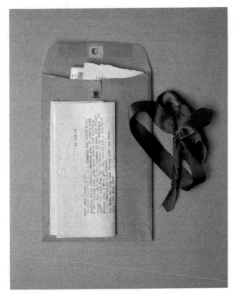

1130

1131

1132

LOT 1130

Vogue article, typewritten letter, and ribbon

An article on fried chicken (four pages) by Jeffrey Steingarten, photocopied and stapled together with a typewritten letter reading in part: *"Wearing the scarf in bed, longing for solid food, craving fried chicken, craving you. It feels like I just kissed you, your face smooth and smelling soapy. You went into the kitchen in your Air France pants and made tea. My apartment is so Hal-less, it misses you, I miss you. Am sending you a ribbon I was wearing as a headband. The bed's too big, the frying pan's too wide, just like Joni says. Hear weather in Prague dismal . . ."* Dimensions vary.

$20–45

LOT 1131

A group of four postcards

Four vintage postcards of Prague, addressed to Lenore. Each contains one word, spelling out *"MISS" "YOU" "VERY" "MUCH."* All 6 x 4 in.

$15–20   (4)

LOT 1132

A series of photographs

Ten prints from Morris's series of one hundred hotel ceilings, which he was hoping to publish as a book. Each 7 x 5 in.

$80–100   (10)

1135

1133

LOT 1133
A collection of hotel card keys
One hundred and fifty hotel card keys, various locations, kept by Morris from his travels on assignment. 2⅛ x 3⅜ in.
$10–20 (150)

LOT 1134
A group of Post-it notes
A group of twelve Post-it notes, reading in Morris's script: *"Gone to the opera / Gone to the races / Gone fishin' / Gone bargain hunting / Back in two hours / Back in a flash / I will return for your soul at 9pm / Do not disturb my hair / Maid, please make up room / Privado Por Favor / On strike! / No matter how much I beg, do not let me out."* 3 x 3 in.
Not illustrated.
$10–20 (12)
Morris would affix these notes to Doolan's computer when he picked her up for lunch.

LOT 1135
A menu
A paper menu from the Oyster Bar restaurant, folded into a fortune-teller game.
$15–20

1136

1137

1138

LOT 1136
A homemade card
A homemade Valentine from Morris to Doolan, posted from Marfa, Texas, February 12, 2004. Card reads: *"Who makes the bed that can't be made / Who is my mirror, who's my blade / When I am rising like a flood / Who feels the pounding in my blood / Nobody / Nobody but you"* (from lyrics to "Nobody" by Paul Simon). 5 x 6 in.
$10–20

LOT 1137
A lock of hair
A lock of Doolan's hair kept by Morris in a jewelry box. 3 x 1½ x 1 in.
$20–30

LOT 1138
A menu
A menu for a Valentine's dinner, hand-drawn by Doolan. Menu reads: *"Oysters Morris / Celery Branches, Ripe Olives / Flounder Ceviche, Lemon Cucumber / Breast of Partridge / Hearts of Artichoke / Camembert Cheese / Marron Doolan Fantaise / Coffee / Wine: Château Musar, 1992."* 7 x 5 in.
$50–65
Included in lot is a note on a Post-it. Reads: *"Dinner was gorgeous. Delicious wine! Thank you. Love xxx H."*

LOT 1139
A wedding invitation
An invitation to the wedding of Rekha Subramanian and Paulo Vitale, April 2, 2003. 6 x 9 in.
Not illustrated.
$10–25
Doolan attended alone, as Morris was working in L.A.

1140

1141

I'm sorry it upset you. I totally forgot! But they look better on you! Call me when you've calmed down. H

LOT 1140

A group of men's sunglasses

Four pairs of sunglasses. One Original Pilot with silver frame and green lenses. One Ray-Ban, aviator style with gold frame and green lenses. One no label, with brown plastic frames and amber lenses. One Stüssy with a black-and-amber plastic frame and brown lenses.

$40–55   (4)

Included is a photograph showing Morris wearing the Original Pilot frames sitting next to an unidentified woman, 4 x 6 in.

LOT 1141

A group of women's sunglasses

Four pairs of sunglasses. One no label, with heart-shaped white plastic frames and brown lenses. One Yves Saint Laurent cat's-eye style with tortoiseshell frames and brown lenses. One no label, gold wire-framed with green plastic lenses. One no label, round blue-framed with brown lenses.

$40–60   (4)

Included is a photograph, 6 x 4 in., showing Doolan wearing the blue-framed pair sitting next to a fountain. Also included is a note on a Post-it, 3 x 3 in., in Morris's script. Reads: *"I'm sorry it upset you. I totally forgot! But they look better on you! Call me when you've calmed down."* The blue-framed pair once belonged to Morris's ex-girlfriend Juliet Blackwood.

1142

LOT 1142
A green cardigan
A green wool cardigan sweater originally belonging to Jason Frank. Cloth patches on elbows. Label inside reads "Cooper & Row Ltd." Size M.
$20–35

Included are two photographs. One snapshot of Morris on couch, wearing the green sweater, 4 x 6 in. One snapshot of Doolan in her apartment, wearing the same sweater, 4 x 6 in.

1143

LOT 1143
A McGill University Athletics T-shirt
A gray cotton McGill University Athletics
T-shirt, emblazoned with varsity logo.
Much wear and fading. Label inside
reads "Russell Athletics." Size XL.
$10–15

Included are two photographs. One snapshot of
Doolan with her computer in bed, wearing the T-
shirt. One snapshot of Morris on a staircase,
wearing the T-shirt. Both 6 x 4 in. The couple
referred to the T-shirt as "the sex T-shirt," as
wearing it indicated a readiness for sex. The shirt
originally belonged to Jared Bristow, an
ex-boyfriend of Doolan's from high school.

55

1144

LOT 1144
A small spiral notebook
A small blue spiral notebook kept by Morris during sessions with Dr. Jay Zaretzsky. Reads in part: *"04.06.04: Father—didn't express love / Mother—too much love / work on being present / even when feel like running away / Don't need to solve her problems / just listen."* 4½ x 2½ in.
$12–25

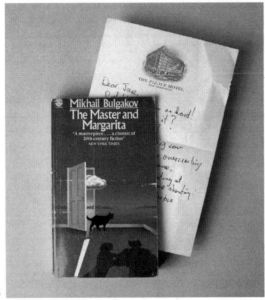

1145

LOT 1145
Bulgakov, Mikhail
The Master and Margarita, paperback edition (Fontana, 1983). Some wear. Laid into front cover is an unsent handwritten letter from Morris to Jason Frank on Palace Hotel, San Francisco, letterhead, reading in part: *"Christ, Jason, big row first thing. Lenore overreacting and throwing my incense, interrupting and shouting at me. Ended up with me shouting: 'STOP SHOUTING!' before fleeing the apartment . . ."* Dimensions vary.
$10–15

LOT 1146
A newspaper clipping
A clipping of Doolan's *Cakewalk* column, dated May 1, 2004, on pineapple upside-down cake. Title: "A Frown Turned Upside Down." Column begins: *"Bright, tropical, sticky, and sweet—nothing banishes a foul mood like pineapple . . ."* 6½ x 2½ in.
Not illustrated.
$5–10

LOT 1147
A group of gray women's clothing
Two jersey T-shirts, no label. One pair gray cigarette pants, label inside reads "Sixes," size 40. One gray long-sleeve T-shirt, label reads "Rick Owens." One gray silk camisole, label reads "Balenciaga," size 38. And one dark gray long-sleeve T-shirt with ribbed sleeves, label reads "Rick Owens," size 40.
$10–30 (6)

1147

1148

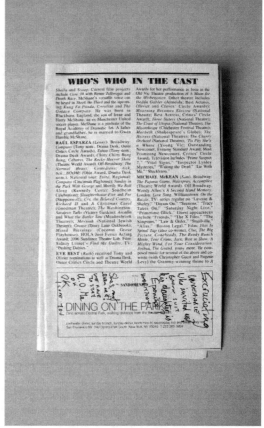

1149

LOT 1148
Munro, Alice

Lives of Girls and Women, paperback (Vintage, 2001). Well-used condition, cover is torn. Laid in is a note from Morris to Doolan. Reads in part: *"I think you're overreacting. I am sorry to have had to miss dinner, truly sorry, and I should have called yes, but it was a work party. Please understand, these functions are boringly important . . ."* Dimensions vary.
$10–15

LOT 1149
A theater program

A playbill from *Les Misérables*. Handwriting in margins alternates between Doolan and Morris: *"Excruciating / Unbearable / Who invited us? / Brown suit / His daughter is Eponine? / Eponine understudy / She's not even in it? / We have to stay / U.O. Me / Ok / Ok / I love you."* 7 x 5 in.
$10–15

LOT 1150
A short handwritten letter

A thank-you note from Ann Doolan to Lenore Doolan, on printer paper. Reads in part: *"Sis, thanks for letting us crash, so pls thank Hal for taking YOU in. I really like him—I think he's a good guy for you. Are things getting more serious? Noticed you'd given him a shelf for Count Chocula (we snuck some). I thought sugary cereal was a total dealbreaker for you! True love?? X, Anny and Tom."* 11 x 8½ in.
Not illustrated.
$10–15

1151

LOT 1151

A group of five hats

A red angora cloche, label reading "Marida." A blue
wool cloche, label reading "Jean Charles Brousseau."
A hat of white fur, label reading "Yves Saint
Laurent." A black straw cap with veil, no label. A
black mesh cap with silk flowers, no label.

$120–160   (5)

Included is a funeral program for Glenda Lucas, Doolan's maternal
grandmother, and five photographs of Doolan wearing the hats, all
6 x 4 in., taken by Morris. The hats belonged to Lucas, who left
them to her granddaughter.

LOT 1152

A Dior scarf

A heavy silk pink scarf, label reading "Christian
Dior." Good condition. Length 23 in.

$40–55

The scarf was left to Doolan by her maternal grandmother, Glenda
Lucas. Lucas had been given the scarf by a man named Lew
Francis, whom she dated seriously before she married Walter
Lucas, Doolan's grandfather. Glenda Lucas remained friendly with
Lew Francis her entire life, and often told Doolan stories about
him.

1152

1154

1155

LOT 1153

A printout of an e-mail containing address information

A printout of an e-mail exchange between Morris and Doolan, reading in full: *From: hmorris256@yahoo.com To: lenore_doolan@nytimes.com Date: June 7, 2004 Subject Re: Re: Bosporus Birthday? That's great! Let me know as soon as you can? X H* On June 6, 2004, at 3:34 PM, lenore_doolan wrote: *Hal, would LOOOOVVEE to but I might need to spend my birthday with my mother. She's still shaky. I'll let you know. X* On June 6, 2004, at 9:08 AM, hmorris256 wrote: *Darling, job has been extended, let me fly you out for a long weekend to spend your birthday with me here? We can sail down the Bosporus, the two of us. My hotel info: Hotel Pera Pelas, Mesrutiyet Cad. No.52, Beyoglu, Istanbul, Turkey 902122430737.*
Not illustrated.
$12–20

LOT 1154

Hammam towels and silver belt

Two Turkish hammam towels, striped. Used, good condition. Unusual antique silver belt with locking clasp. Good condition. Dimensions vary.
$40–90   (3)

LOT 1155

An agenda

A Smythson of Bond Street Day-to-a-page Diary, 2004. June 19 page reads: *"Bread and honey / Turkish coffee / Olives / Kofte / Club Sandwich / Red wine"* Facing page, June 20, reads: *"Drove to a small mosque, then to Sofia palace, bought a belt. Hal slept till 4. Sweet-faced . . . What am I doing here? I should be home. I should be with Mom. Hate hotels, hate wandering between meals, hate feeling overstuffed, hate the tiny pieces of soap, hate the telephones in the toilets. What am I doing here? Homesick. Does everything have to be on his terms? Sex on his terms. Telephone conversations on his terms. Is he who I need? Am I who he needs? Does he need everybody? Does he need anybody? Does he need me? Why doesn't he know when I need him? Why doesn't he know what to do when he knows I need him? I would miss Hal. I would miss Sherman St. I would miss the mornings. I love his head. I love his eyes (when open). I love his mind. I love his legs. I hate his sullenness. I hate his arrogance. I hate his drinking. I hate his drinking. I hate his double standard. What do I want?"* 7½ x 5½ in.
$15–25

LOT 1156

An invitation and a program

An invitation to the National Newspaper Awards. Doolan was nominated for her *New York Times* story about blancmange. 6 x 6 in.
Not illustrated.
$10–15
As Doolan was in Istanbul, she could not attend the awards ceremony.

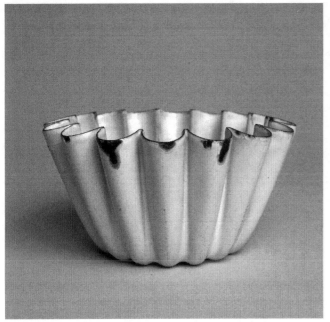

1157

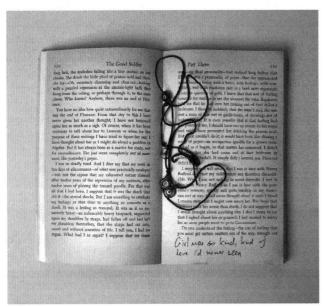

1159

1158

LOT 1157

A blancmange mold

A blancmange mold given to Morris by Doolan, used for holding exposed film. 6 in. diam. x 4¼ in. tall.

$10–20

LOT 1158

A Tate Modern museum program

A museum program for a Luc Tuymans retrospective at the Tate Modern attended by Morris prior to traveling to Istanbul. 6½ x 5¼ in.

$10–20

Marking page 14 is a hair clip of Doolan's, purchased in Symi.

LOT 1159

Ford, Ford Madox; Turkish evil-eye bracelet

The Good Soldier, paperback edition (Vintage Books, 1955). Some wear and yellowing to pages. Written in ballpoint pen on back inside cover in Morris's script are the lyrics to the song "Wined and Dined" by Syd Barrett, reading in part: *"Girl was so kind / kind of love I'd never seen . . ."* Laid in is a Turkish evil-eye charm bracelet. Dimensions vary.

$10–20

1160

1161

LOT 1160

Notes

Handwritten notes on a page torn out of *Tate Etc.* magazine, Summer 2004. Reading: *"Chipotle penne recipe from Natasha / Call ob-gyn / Herbs Chinatown for Hal / Soda bread recipe / Cornbread deadline / Ask Jess about ayurvedic derm for Hal / Book on homeopathy / Omega-3s / 2 slices toast / Sm avocado salad / Cheese and crackers / Ham sandwich / Tea / Kit Kat."* 8 x 10⅜ in. (unfolded).

$10–15

LOT 1161

A pair of photographs

One of Doolan washing dishes. One of Doolan reading on the lawn. Both taken by Morris at Orient Point, Long Island. 4 x 6 in.

$10–15   (2)

Doolan is seen wearing striped dress from Lot 1069, hat from Lot 1229, and bathing suit from Lot 1092.

LOT 1162

A cookbook and a postcard

A cookbook titled *Irish Countryhouse Cooking* by Rosie Tinne (Weathervane Books, 1974). A postcard, dated August 29, 2004, from Morris in Ireland to Doolan. Image on front is a painting by James O'Connor of the Delphi Lodge and Finn Lough, 1818, in county Mayo. The card reads in full: *"I want to live here."* 9¼ x 6⅜ in. (cb), 4½ x 6 in. (pc).

$12–18

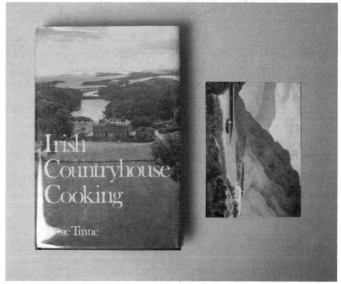

1162

1164

LOT 1163

A fax

A fax from Glin Castle to *The New York Times*, dated September 7, 2004. Reads in full: *"So excited you're coming—one small deet: we now won't be in Dublin till the 11th. Shoot in Galway running longer, but wait for me! Please come to Harrogate with me too? Love Hal xxx."* 11 x 8½ in.

Not illustrated.

$15–20

LOT 1164

A pair of tweed suits

A pair of tweed two-piece suits, one men's size 48, one women's size 36, tailored by William F. Frazer, Hospital, county Limerick.

$80–100   (2)

LOT 1165
Nathan, Monique
Virginia Woolf, paperback edition (Grove Press, 1961). Laid in is a handwritten letter from Ann Doolan to Lenore Doolan, dated September 15, 2004. Reads in part: *"Dinner with his mother sounds like a nightmare. How did she correct your speech exactly? Did Hal defend you . . . ?"* Pale pink G. Lalo, Vergé de France paper. 8 x 5¾ in.
$10–20

LOT 1166
A toast rack and an envelope containing baby teeth
A ceramic Seven Dwarves toast rack (chips and losses). A small envelope marked "Tim's Teeth" in faded fountain pen script. 8 in. in length (toast rack), 5½ x 3½ in. (env.).
$18–22
Given to Morris by his mother, Eleanor. The teeth belonged to Morris's late father, Timothy Morris, and the toast rack was from Morris's childhood home.

LOT 1167
A handwritten letter
A handwritten letter from Eleanor Morris to Hal Morris, dated September 17, 2004. Reads in part: *"Lovely to meet Lenore after hearing so much about her. She's quite young, I'm afraid I WAS a bore. Where is she from in Canada? Dr. Hauchukova is fine, I do like him, and the medications seem to be agreeing with me. It's only I'm very tired all the time . . ."* On pale blue airmail stationery, 10 x 7 in.
Not illustrated.
$10–20

LOT 1168
A newspaper clipping
A newspaper clipping of Doolan's *Cakewalk* column, dated September 29, 2004, on Guinness cake. Title: "All about Stout." Column begins: *"Rich, dark, and bitter can be intimidating qualities in a woman, but rather nice in a cake . . ."*
Not illustrated.
$5–10

1165

1166

1169

1170

LOT 1169
An invitation
An invitation to a Halloween party, October 31, 2004, given by Morris's close friends Rekha Subramanian and Paulo Vitale. 5¼ x 4 in.

$5–10

Included in lot is a snapshot of Doolan and Morris in Halloween costumes. Doolan is dressed as Anna Magnani, Morris as Paddington Bear. Photographer unknown. 4 x 6 in.

LOT 1170
A blue vase
A blue vase, engraved with signature "McCoy USA." Given by Morris to Doolan, with roses, as an anniversary present (chips and losses). Height 9 in.

$40–55

Doolan later noted in her diary that the roses did not open.

LOT 1171
A pair of cufflinks and a card
A pair of airplane cufflinks given by Doolan to Morris on Thanksgiving 2004. Accompanied by a homemade card, reading: *"Favorite Moments of the Year: / 1. When you went into the closet to spare me. / 2. The time you walked me to my door even though you were late. / 3. Watching the way you pack. / 4. When you called the man at Craft a dirtbag. / 5. When you switched places with me at Toby's dinner. / 6. Your about-to-laugh face."* 6 x 3½ in.
Not illustrated.

$10–20

1172

LOT 1172
A travel clock

An Elgin travel clock, including original box. Given to Morris by Doolan.

$40–60

Doolan insisted that the clock remain on New York time. Morris took the clock on two trips, but complained that it was too heavy.

1173

LOT 1173
Plath, Sylvia

Johnny Panic and the Bible of Dreams (Harper & Row, 1978), first edition. Good condition. Laid into the short story "The Fifty-ninth Bear," page 105, is a scrap of yellow foolscap paper with a short handwritten list in Doolan's hand: *"Batteries / Scotch tape/ watermelon / Guacamole / Pros: / travel / talk of family, names / Cons: / insensitive / defensive / doesn't dance / fake laugh? / doesn't want a dog."* 9½ x 6½ x 1⅛ in. (book); 8 x 6 in. (note).

$20–45

1174

LOT 1174
A half a wishbone

The winning side of a turkey wishbone. Kept by Morris in his bedside table. Length 3½ in.

$5–10

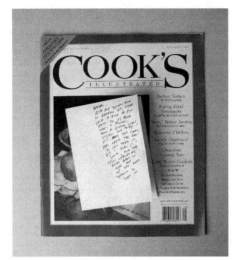

1175

1176

1177

LOT 1175

Cook's Illustrated

A December 2004 issue of *Cook's Illustrated*. Laid in is an invitation to the Bainbridge-Polarski Christmas party. On reverse is written: *"Dream. Blue and yellow bird in parking lot, dead with a blob of pink next to its body. Then a pigeon, and a black crow, inside the house, but not the room. Hal opens the door to let them in, but I slam it shut, and the crow wedges his beak in the top of the door, trying to get in."* 5 x 5 in.
$10–20

LOT 1176

A handwritten note

A Chase Manhattan withdrawal receipt. On reverse in Morris's script is written, *"Do you still want a boyfriend?"* beneath which is written, in Doolan's script, *"Yes, I want a boyfriend with blue eyes,"* followed by, in Morris's script, *"And I want an unpredictable girlfriend."* 5¾ x 3¼ in.
$10–20

LOT 1177

Six jars of homemade strawberry jam

Six jars of homemade strawberry jam, made by Doolan to give as joint Christmas gifts from the couple. Labels read: *"Tidings of Comfort and Jam, Love From Hal and Lenore"* and *"Have A Berry Christmas, Love From Hal and Lenore."*
$20–45 (6)

66

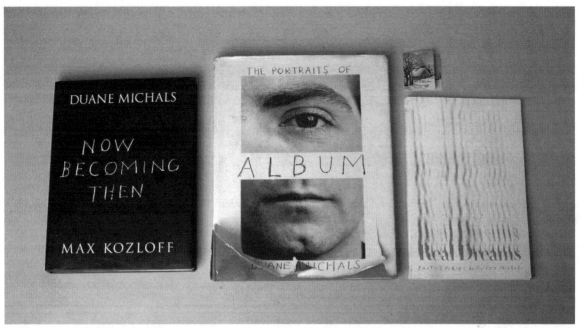

1178

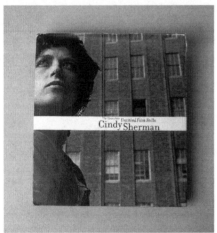

1179

1180

LOT 1178
Michals, Duane

A collection of Duane Michals photography books, including *Now Becoming Then* (Twin Palms, 1990); *Album: The Portraits of Duane Michals* (Twelvetree Press, 1988); *Real Dreams, Photo Stories* (Addison House, 1976). Inscription in *Album* from Doolan to Morris reads: *"More from your hero. Love L, Merry Christmas."* Dimensions vary.
$200–400   (3)

LOT 1179
Sherman, Cindy

The Complete Untitled Film Stills (Museum of Modern Art, 2003), hardcover first edition. Fair condition, some wear and earmarking to pages. Inscribed by Morris to Doolan: *"She reminds me of you . . . Merry Xmas 2004, love Hal."*
9¾ x 11 in.
$25–30

LOT 1180
A Hasselblad camera

A Hasselblad 500 C/M single-lens reflex medium-format camera. Used, in good condition. Given by Morris to Doolan, Christmas 2004.
$400–500

1181

1182

LOT 1181

Poodle figurines and playbill

Two antique poodle figurines, one with a small chain
collar. Height, 3 in. Included in lot is a playbill for
Wonderful Town. Handwriting in margins alternates
between Morris and Doolan: *"I can tell you hate them
/ No! / But I love the dogs, the dogs love you, they are
perfect pets, as they do not poo. / Dearest Hal, they are not
our pal, their breed is a pain, a firm hand must train. /
Lenore, Lenore, fear not evermore, these unbroken pups
you'll soon adore. / You win, dark knight, at least they
don't bite."*
$15–20   (3)

LOT 1182

An invitation

An invitation to a New Year's Eve party thrown by
Rekha Subramaniam and Paulo Vitale. 6½ x 4¾ in.
$10–20

LOT 1183

A newspaper clipping

A newspaper clipping of Doolan's *Cakewalk* column,
dated January 8, 2005, on oliebollen. Title:
"Doughnuts for Mid-Winter's Evil Spirits." 7½ x 2½ in.
Not illustrated.
$5–10

1184

LOT 1184

Kitto, H.D.F.; a postcard

Greek Tragedy (Doubleday Anchor, 1955). Laid in is a postcard of the photograph "En Route to New Orleans" by William Eggleston, postmarked February 8, 2005, from Athens, Greece. Verso reads: *"Lenore, I am hoping beyond hope that I will be back for Valentine's chez vous. Keep your fingers crossed the magazine will be fine with everything. Expect a case of wine in advance of me! Lovingly, Hal xx."* 6 x 4 in.
$10–20

LOT 1185

A collection of rocks

Rocks collected by Morris from various locations, kept on the windowsill at 11A Sherman Street. Sizes vary.
$10–20   (5)

1185

1186

LOT 1186

Two bottles of wine

Two bottles of Château Calon-Ségur, Saint-Estèphe, 1989.

$55–95

Morris sent Doolan a case of this wine for Valentine's Day 2005. A note affixed (but since lost) suggested she move in with him.

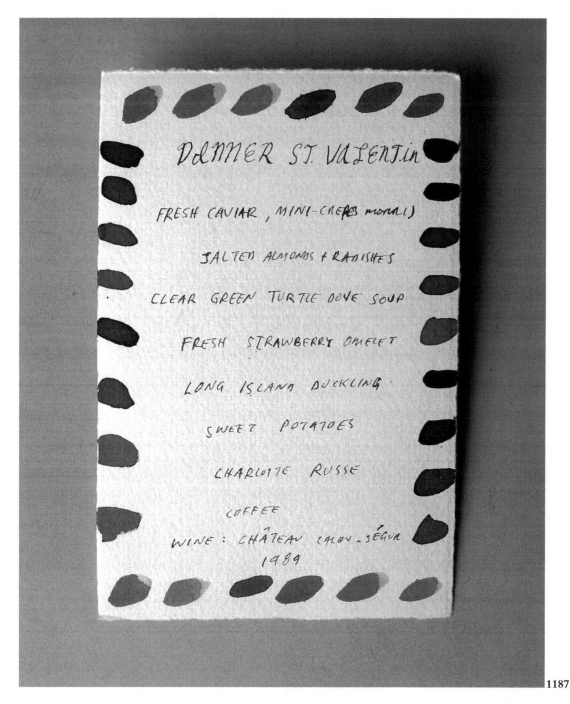

DINNER ST. VALENTIN

FRESH CAVIAR , MINI-CREPES MORRIS)

SALTED ALMONDS + RADISHES

CLEAR GREEN TURTLE DOVE SOUP

FRESH STRAWBERRY OMELET

LONG ISLAND DUCKLING

SWEET POTATOES

CHARLOTTE RUSSE

COFFEE

WINE : CHÂTEAU CALON-SÉGUR
1989

1187

LOT 1187

A menu

A menu for a Valentine's dinner, hand-drawn by Doolan. Doolan invited Morris to dine at her apartment upon his arrival from Athens that day. Menu reads: *"Fresh caviar, mini-crepes Morris / Salted almonds & radishes / Clear green turtle dove soup / Fresh strawberry omelet / Long Island duckling / Sweet potatoes / Charlotte Russe / Coffee / Wine: Château Calon-Ségur 1989."* 6¾ x 4½ in.

$50–65

1188

1189

LOT 1188
A selection of men's pants

Four pairs of men's pants. One pair of vintage tan corduroys, label inside reading "Levi's Gentleman's Jeans." One pair of dark green cotton, label inside reading "Costume National," size 50. One pair of navy pin corduroy, label inside reading "Helmut Lang." And one pair of striped gray cotton, label inside reading "Dries Van Noten," size 50.

$150–195 (4)

All were gifts from Doolan to Morris after his luggage was stolen out of his car parked in front of Doolan's apartment during Valentine's Day dinner.

LOT 1189
A Tiffany key ring

A sterling silver Tiffany key ring. Some wear and scratches. Included is original box. 1½ in. in width.

$50–65

Given by Morris to Doolan with a set of keys to 11A Sherman Street. Engraved tag, barely legible, reads "L."

1190

LOT 1190
A silver–plated cup

A cup used by the couple for their toothbrushes. 5½ in. in height.

$15–25

Included in lot is a snapshot of the cup in the bathroom at 11A Sherman Street.

LOT 1191
A framed postcard

A vintage postcard of the St. Regis Hotel. 7¼ x 5¼ in.

$10–15

1191

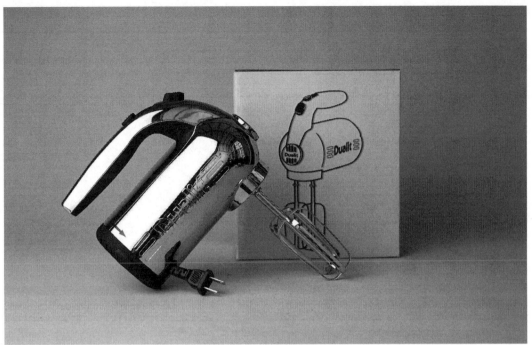

1192

1193

LOT 1192

A mixer

A Dualit five-speed deluxe mixer. Used, good condition.
$12–15

LOT 1193

A set of Martini glasses and a book

A set of vintage art deco martini glasses. A cocktail recipe book from 1933. The inscription in the book reads: *"For my hard-drinkin' Hal, with love from your new roomie. Lenore xx."* Dimensions vary.
$40–60 (5)

1195

1196

LOT 1194

A newspaper clipping

A clipping of Doolan's *Cakewalk* column, dated March 25, 2005, on cassata Siciliana. Title: "A House of Sponge and Cream." Column begins: *"Think Hansel and Gretel's dream home, minus the witch . . ."* 8½ x 2½ in.
Not illustrated.
$5–10

LOT 1195

A cake stand

A porcelain cake stand. Used, good condition. 5 in. in height by 9 in. in diameter.
$12–15

LOT 1196

A series of photographs of cake

Six photographs on Polaroid Polacolor ER 669 film, taken by Doolan of various homemade cakes. 4¼ x 3¼ in.
$12–25   (6)

1197

1198

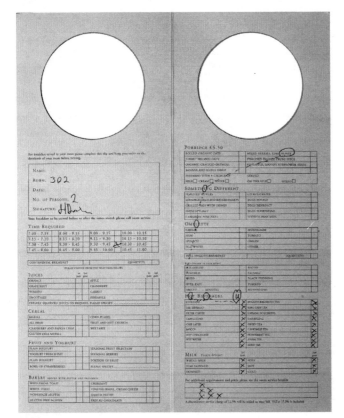

1199

LOT 1197
A small headlamp
A halogen headlamp, affixed with an elasticized cloth band.
$12–15
Used by Doolan for reading in bed.

LOT 1198
Two framed photographs
A pair of framed black-and-white photographs, one of Doolan's beloved childhood pet dog, Shiny Eyes, and one of Morris's beloved childhood pet hamster, Herbert. Pressed into frame are two photobooth prints of the couple.
Dimensions vary.
$20–30   (2)

LOT 1199
A breakfast menu
A doorknob menu from a hotel, left for Doolan at 11A Sherman Street, marked with a note from Morris to Doolan spelling out: *"HONEY, I LOVE YOU, XXXXXXXXXXX"* 11½ x 4½ in.
$10–20

1201

LOT 1200 removed.

LOT 1201
Bowles, Jane
A French–language paperback edition of *Deux dames sérieuses* (10/18, 1969).
Laid in are five photographs of Doolan's ex–boyfriends.
$5–10   (6)

1202

LOT 1202

Books on cooking from Doolan's library

Twenty-three volumes on cooking and cookbooks, including *Cakes, Regional and Traditional* by Julie Duff (Grub Street, 2003); *Chez Panisse Desserts* by Lindsey Remolif Shere (Random House, 1994); *How to Be a Domestic Goddess* by Nigella Lawson (Hyperion, 2002); *The Art of Fine Baking* by Paula Peck (Gallahad, 1961); *Delia Smith: How to Cook,* book one (DK Adult, 2002); *Tamasin's Weekend Food* by Tamasin Day Lewis (Weidenfeld and Nicholson, 2004); *Just Desserts* by Jeni Wright (Sundial, 1980); *Images à la Carte* by Claes Oldenburg (Paula Cooper, 2004); M.F.K. Fisher's translation of Brillat-Savarin's *Physiology of Taste* (Knopf, 1971); *Mexican Cookbook* by Erna Fergusson (University of New Mexico Press, 1945); *Cooking Made Easy* by Anna Lee Scott (Maple Leaf Milling Co., 1947); *Pies and Tarts,* Williams Sonoma Kitchen Library (Time Life Books, 1999); *Simple French Cookery* by Edna Beilenson (Peter Pauper Press, 1958); *Modern Cookery Illustrated* by Lydia Chatterton (Odhams Press, 1947); *The Moro Cookbook* by Sam and Sam Clark (Ebury Press, 2003); *Nigel Slater Appetite* (Fourth Estate, 2002); *The Gourmet Cookbook* (Houghton Mifflin, 2004); *Modern Greek* by Andy Harris (Chronicle, 2002); *The Joy of Cooking* by Irma Rombauer, Marion Rombauer Becker, and Ethan Becker (Simon & Schuster, 1997); *Tea and Sympathy Cookbook* by Anita Naughton (Putnam, 2002); *The River Café Cookbook* by Rose Grey and Ruth Rogers (Ebury Press, 1996); *Beard on Bread* by James Beard (Knopf, 1995); *Dining with Proust* by Jean Bernard Naudin (Random House, 1992).

$80–105   (23)

1203

LOT 1203

Books on photography from Morris's library

Forty volumes of photography books, including *Weegee's People* by Alfred "Weegee" Fellig (De Capo Press, 1985); *Women* by Richard Prince (Regen Projects/Hatje Cantz Verlag, 2004); *Fragments from the Real World* by Garry Winogrand (Harry N. Abrams, 1988); *End of an Age* by Paul Graham (Scalo, 1999); *Strangers and Friends* by Thomas Struth (MIT Press, 1994); *William Eggleston 2¼* (Twelvetree Press, 1999); *All of a Sudden* by Jack Pierson (D.A.P., 1995); *Teenage Lust* by Larry Clark (Larry Clark, 1983); *Fashion: Photography of the Nineties* (Scalo, 1998); *David Hockney Photographs* (Petersburg Press, 1992); *The Bikeriders* by Danny Lyon (Twin Palms Publishers, 1998); *Jeff Wall* (Scalo, 1997); *Man Ray, Paris L.A.* (D.A.P., 1997); *Mamarazza* (Steidl, 1999); *Carlo Mollino Photographs, 1956–1962* (Salon 94, 2005); *Les Femmes* by J. H. Lartigue (Dutton & Co., 1974); *Like a One-Eyed Cat* by Lee Friedlander (Seattle Art Museum, 1989); *Nudes* by Thomas Ruff (Harry N. Abrams, 2003); *Boris Mikhailikov: A Retrospective* (Scalo, 2003); *The Lonely Life* by Jack Pierson (Edition Stemmele, 1997); *Babyland* by Takashi Homma (Littlemore, 1995); *Wolfgang Tillmans* (Taschen, 2002); *Sweet Life* by Ed van der Elsken (Harry N. Abrams, 1966). Laid in to *Weegee's People* is a vintage card from Doolan to Morris reading: *"You . . . I like."*

$1000–1500 (40)

1204

LOT 1204

Duplicate paperbacks

Duplicate copies of seven paperbacks, including *This Side of Paradise* by F. Scott Fitzgerald (Penguin, 1978, and Scribner, 1960); *Bleak House* by Charles Dickens (Bantam, 1983, and Signet, 1964); *The Comedians* by Graham Greene (Penguin, 1966 and 1976); *Notes from Underground* by Fyodor Dostoevesky (Dutton, 1960, and Penguin, 1972); *The White Hotel* by D. M. Thomas (Penguin, 1993, and King Penguin, 1982); *The Loser* by Thomas Bernhard (Vintage, 1993 and 2004); *The End of the Affair* by Graham Greene (Penguin, 1979 and 2004). Conditions vary. Dimensions vary.

$60–70   (14)

1205

LOT 1205
A group of baking pamphlets
Eight baking pamphlets from Doolan's collection.
Conditions and sizes vary.

$10–20

(8)

LOT 1205a
A card table
A card table covered in visitor's pass stickers. 27 x 27 x 36 in. high.

Not illustrated.

$40–60

Upon returning home from business meetings, Morris would routinely stick his visitor's passes to the surface of this table.

1206

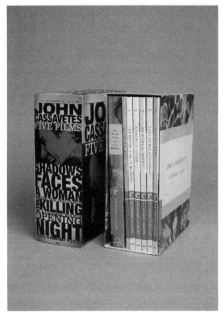

1207

1208

LOT 1206
A group of socks
Seven pairs of socks, lightly worn. Label in all reads "Paul Smith."

$10–30 (7)

Morris had a habit of wearing two pairs of socks every day: one pair he considered "inside" socks, worn inside a pair of dressier "outside" socks, usually Paul Smith.

LOT 1207
Two boxed sets of DVDs
One boxed set of John Cassavetes films and one boxed set of Eric Rohmer films.

$40–60

The boxed sets were given by Doolan to Morris. The DVD *Claire's Knee* is missing from the Rohmer set.

LOT 1208
A framed photograph
A framed black-and-white still of Monica Vitti from *L'Avventura*. 11 x 9 in.

$10–15

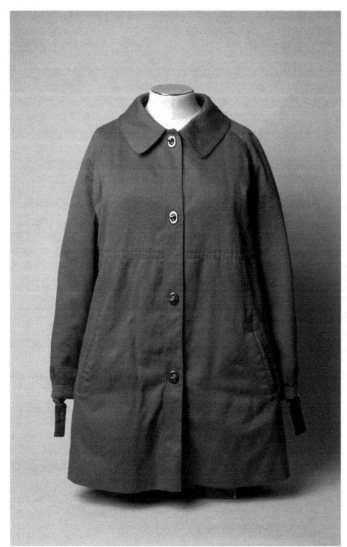

1209

1210

1211

LOT 1209
A women's jacket
A red lined jacket, label reading "Weatherbee Fashion Original." Women's size 5. A shopping list in the jacket pocket—in Doolan's script with the last three items in Morris's script—reads: *"Maldon sea salt / agave / pancetta / asparagus / pea shoots / Devon cream / seedless raspberry jam / caster sugar / white peppercorns / semolina flour / plum tomatoes / speck / Frosted Flakes / Goober Grape / Diet Coke."* 5 x 7 in.
$10–20

LOT 1210
A group of takeout menus
Ten identical takeout menus from local Chinese restaurant Wah-Sing. Circled in all are Sautéed Mustard Greens, General Zao's Chicken, Scallion Pancake, Health Special Baby Bok Choy, and Brown Rice. 17 x 11 in. (unfolded).
$5–10   (10)

LOT 1211
A coffee grinder
A vintage KitchenAid coffee grinder. Some wear and staining. 12½ in. in height.
$25–30

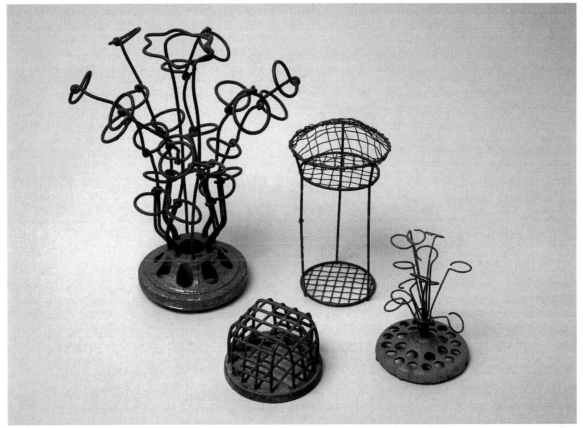

1212

LOT 1212
Cast-iron flower frogs
Four green cast-iron flower frogs, some chipping to paint on bases. Conditions and sizes vary.
$5–10   (4)

LOT 1213
Easter eggs
A collection of eleven hand-dyed Easter eggs, decorated by the couple. Some cracked, some fading.
$10–20   (11)

LOT 1214
A newspaper clipping
A clipping of Doolan's *Cakewalk* column, dated May 19, 2005, on hot cross buns. Title: "One a Penny, Two a Penny." Column begins: *"While I am not the most devout Catholic, I still observe a few irresistible Easter traditions . . ."* 8⅛ x 2½ in.
Not illustrated.

$5–10

1213

LOT 1215

A box of Trivial Pursuit question cards

Some wear to the edges of the box and the corners of the cards. Kept in the bathroom at 11A Sherman Street and read from while the couple performed their morning and evening ablutions.

$20–25

1215

LOT 1216

A handwritten note

A handwritten note from Doolan to Morris, written on the back of a printout of a recipe for simnel cake. Reads in part: *"I just couldn't believe you said you were fucking sick of cake. This is my livelihood, and it really hurt my feelings. I understand you can be tired of being my guinea pig, but I'm starting to feel deep down that you don't appreciate what I do or care about it. It's like you don't value who I am. My job is just as hard as yours."* 11 x 8½ in. *Not illustrated.*

$10–20

LOT 1217

Delacorta

Three paperbacks: *Luna* (Ballantine, 1985); *Nana* (Ballantine, 1987); and *Diva* (Ballantine, 1988). Laid in to *Nana* is a handwritten letter from Morris to Doolan, written on lined notepaper. Reads: *"7.50 am: The train left five minutes late. Am seated behind an attractive couple. He is wearing an ordinary T-shirt and cool jeans, she has a pretty American face, ponytail. I think they are in love. 10 am: I have never taken the train beyond Poughkeepsie. 11 am: The couple are sleeping on each other. I heard them kiss and smiled into my novel. I wonder if you will pick me up at the station? Hope so. 1 pm (slept through 12): Patchy fields under a cold sky. Where is spring? The train has stopped. The intercom crackles, and the conductor's voice: 'Ladies and Gentlemen, your attention please, somebody was struck by a train ahead of us. There has been a fatality, as soon as the body has been cleared we will proceed.' Christ. 2 pm: Lunch, cheese sandwich, carrot, and two minibottles of wine. 4 pm: Utica. 6 pm: Just leaving Niagara Falls. Need coffee. xx H."* In May 2005 Morris took the train to visit Doolan's family in Guelph, Ontario, where Doolan's father was in the hospital undergoing a kidney operation. Dimensions vary.

$10–20   (3)

Included is a draft of a handwritten note from Morris to Doolan's mother, Tracey, apologizing for his early departure. Reads in part: *"Dear Tracey, I am so sorry to have to cut my visit short. I am so glad to have seen you and thank you for the muffins . . ."*

1217

1219

1220

LOT 1218 removed.

LOT 1219
A group of objects
Presents sent by Morris to Doolan
while he was on an advertising job
for Volvo in Australia, Japan, Paris,
Germany, and Morocco. *Yamanote*
by Inigo Asis (Pocko Editions,
2001). One leather air freshener.
One blue Fouquet candy tin with
pink ribbon. One kangaroo-fur
purse. One pair of Austrian
undershorts. One miniature Eiffel
tower. One package mint candies.
$30–40   (7)

LOT 1220
**A series of photographs of
refrigerator interiors**
Four photographs on Polaroid
Polacolor ER 669 film taken by
Doolan of various interiors of
friends' refrigerators. 3¼ x 4¼ in.
$12–25   (4)

LOT 1221

A printout of an e-mail exchange

A printout of an e-mail exchange between Morris in Brussels to Doolan in New York, dated June 6, 2005. Reads: *From: hmorris256@yahoo.com* *To: lenore_doolan@nytimes.com* *Date: June 6, 2005/ Subject: re: YOU* *Terrific one, thank you for your kind words, I look forward to our reunion. Pls do not think me suggestive in proposing that I put my nuts on your honey cake.* *Flight info: Delta 908 arriving JFK at 1600 06/06/05.* On June 5, 2005, at 3:14 PM, lenore_doolan wrote: *Sweetheart you sounded so low on the phone. I don't think you should ever underestimate the fact that you have mastered a skill, that you have trained and sure, what you do doesn't exactly save lives but you do your bit, it shapes culture. You are so well respected in your trade, highly paid, and you have something to offer. The bad jobs are finite and the good ones are rewarding, no? Try not to be so hard on yourself, blow your per diem on a good steak dinner. (Look at me! I write about cake. Cake. Totally useless! I romanticize the '50s housewife! I give people cavities!) Speaking of, come over as soon as you get in, I've been trying out a Greek honey cake recipe and have tons left over. Xx.*

11 x 8½ in.

Not illustrated.

$5–10

1222

LOT 1222

A pair of bedside lamps

A lamp from Lenore's side of the couple's bed, with a round green ceramic base and white shade. A lamp from Morris's side of the bed, with three iron legs supporting a yellow ceramic base, and a tan shade. Dimensions vary.

$50–70   (2)

LOT 1223

A group of photographs

One black-and-white print of Celadon House, 5 x 7 in. One color photograph of Morris walking across a lawn, 4 x 6 in. One color photograph of Doolan standing on front steps, 6 x 4 in.

$20–30   (3)

The couple rented Celadon in upstate New York for the summers of 2004 and 2005.

1223

1224

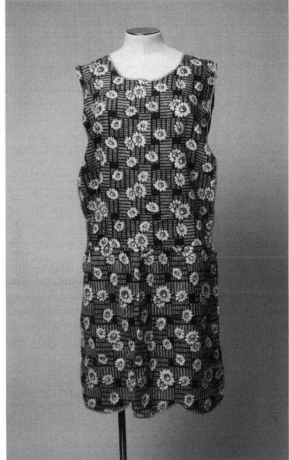

1225

LOT 1224
Two aprons
One red-and-white striped cotton, label reads "Daniel Boulud Kitchens." One vintage flower print, no label. Laid into pocket of latter is a note on the back of a shopping list handwritten from Morris to Doolan. Reads in full: *"Dear one, Third batch of macaroons definitely the best. X."* 7 x 2 in. Both aprons size small.
$5–10
Included in lot is a photograph of Doolan in the striped apron.

LOT 1225
Burnt sage
A burnt wand of sage.
$5–10
Doolan thought she saw a ghost in the dining room of Celadon House and had trouble sleeping. Morris fumigated the room with sage in an effort to make her more comfortable.

1226

LOT 1226
A group of tag-sale items
A Kodak towel. A stainless-steel ice cream scoop. A 1940s cotton baby onesie, price tag still attached, reading: $35. A pair of hot and cold faucet knobs. One pair gray men's garters. *Understanding Human Behavior: An Illustrated Guide to Successful Human Relationships* (BPC Publishing, 1974). Dimensions vary.

$10–15   (7)

LOT 1227
Lowell, Robert
Five volumes of poetry: *Notebook* (Farrar, Straus and Giroux, 1995); *For Lizzie and Harriet* (Farrar, Straus and Giroux, 1975); *The Dolphin* (Farrar, Straus and Giroux, 1974); *Life Studies* and *For the Union Dead* (Farrar, Straus and Giroux, 1967); and *Lord Weary's Castle* (Meridian, 1966). Dimensions vary.

$10–25   (5)

1227

1228

1229

LOT 1228
Men's summer hats
Two straw fedoras. No labels, some wear.
$40–55   (2)

LOT 1229
Women's summer hats
Two cotton sunhats. One gingham, good condition, the
other in a Marimekko pattern, no labels, wear to brim.
$40–55   (2)

1230

LOT 1230
A men's jacket and a fleece sweater

A navy blue seersucker jacket, label reads "Club Monaco." A dark gray fleece, label reads "Vexed Generation." In jacket pocket is a shopping list from Doolan to Morris reading: *"eggs / whipping cream / white caster sugar from D&Deluca, not Domino!"* Both size M.

$80–100

1231

LOT 1231

Two pairs of white shoes

Two pairs of white bucks. The label inside the men's pair reads "Prada," the women's reads "Toast." Sizes men's 11, women's 9. Well worn.

$40–60 (2)

LOT 1232

A brown mug

A broken brown glazed mug stamped "Brickett Davda Made in England" on base.

$5–7

Included in lot is a note handwritten by Doolan. Reads: *"H I'm so sorry, I know this was your favorite. Will get it fixed, I promise."*

1232

LOT 1233

A chocolate box

A chocolate box marked "Les Langues de Chat, Demel Vienne." Laid in is a hair clip, an aluminum pencil sharpener, and a small note from Morris to Doolan reading: *"L, I love your langues and your chat, last night was amazing. x H."*

5¼ x 3¾ x ½ in.

$10–20

1233

1235

1236

LOT 1234
A series of photographs
Twenty photographs, taken by Morris, of his feet at the
end of the bathtub. 5 x 5 in.
Not illustrated.
$60–70   (20)

LOT 1235
A group of eight books
Eight books of erotica: *Sisters* by David Hamilton and Alain
Robbe-Grillet (William Morrow, 1973); *David Hamilton's
Private Collection* (Morrow Quill, 1980); *Dreams of a Young
Girl* by David Hamilton (William Morrow, 1971); *Bilitis* by
David Hamilton (Quill, 1977); *Sleepless Nights* by Helmut
Newton (Congreve, 1978); *Aline et Valcour* by D.A.F. de Sade
(Jean Jacques Pauvert, 1956); *Five Men* by Tiffany Boots
(Venus Library, 1969); *Bed Manners* by Dr. Ralph Hopton
and Anne Balliol (Arden Book Company, 1942).
$60–90   (8)

LOT 1236
Two neckties and two kimono belts
Two vintage striped neckties, tied in slipknots, and two
kimono belts. Lengths vary.
$10–20   (4)

1237

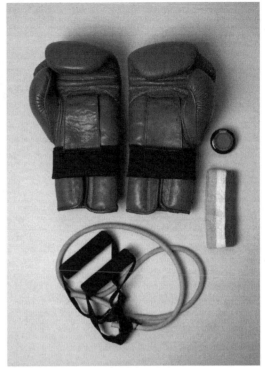

1238

1240

LOT 1237
A group of clothing
One vintage Victorian garter vest. One pair ladies equestrian underwear, no label. One pair unused size C black fishnet stockings in original Agent Provocateur package. One pair transparent plastic high heels, label reading "Private Collection." One pair black high heel shoes, label reading "Christian Louboutin," size 8½.

$70–85 (5)

LOT 1238
A group of exercise equipment
A pair of blue boxing gloves. An odometer. One striped sweatband; label reads "Goorin." Resistance cords. All in used condition.

$20–30 (4)

LOT 1239
A newspaper clipping
A clipping of Doolan's *Cakewalk* column, dated May 31, 2004, on singing hinnie. Title: "Stovetop Melodies." Column begins: *"If singing for your supper is humiliating, turn the tables and have your supper sing for you! . . ."* 9 x 2½ in. *Not illustrated.*

$5–10

LOT 1240
A heart–shaped ice cube mold
A mold in tempered silicon with twelve heart-shaped ice cube forms. Some wear to underside, otherwise good condition. 4⅛ x 8¼ x 1 in.

$5–10

1241

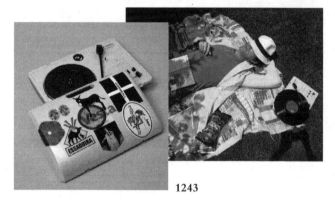

1243

1242

LOT 1241
Bemelmans, Ludwig; Mason, Betty

The Woman of My Life by Ludwig Bemelmans (Hamish Hamilton, 1957); *Dinners That Wait* by Betty Mason (Doubleday and Co., 1957), hardcover, first edition. Good condition, some chips in dust jacket. Laid into second book is a homemade birthday card from Morris to Doolan, reading: *"Violets are red, Roses are blue, When all is said, and done, I love you. Happy Birthday Butterbum. Love Hal."* Also attached is original ribbon and card from Jane Stubbs Books at Bergdorf Goodman. Dimensions vary.
$50–100   (2)

LOT 1242
Elsa Schiaparelli astrakhan coat

A vintage Elsa Schiaparelli astrakhan coat. Some wear on shoulders. Size 36.

$900–1000

Morris found the coat in an Athens secondhand store; the owner assured him that it had once belonged to Maria Callas.

LOT 1243
A record player

A Vestax Handy Trax portable record player. Some wear to case, exterior featuring stickers from various travel destinations. 10¼ x 14½ x 4 in.

$20–30

Included in lot is a photograph taken by Doolan of Morris picnicking with the turntable. Morris is seen wearing hat from Lot 1228. 4 x 6 in.

1245

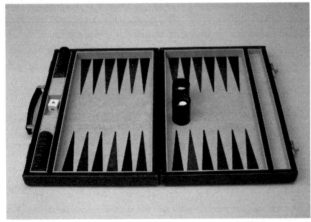

1246

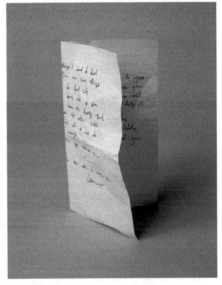

1247

LOT 1244
Brontë, Charlotte
Wuthering Heights, paperback edition (Dover, 1996). Some wear. Laid in as a bookmark is a fortune-cookie reading: *"Your everlasting patience will be rewarded sooner or later."* In the margin of page 105 is scrawled in Doolan's hand: *"Iced coffee / apple / iced coffee / green tea / hamburger w/out bun / vodka tonic."* On margin of page 225 is written in ballpoint ink: *"Sandra's shrink— Midge Zilkha get number."*
Not illustrated.
$12–18

LOT 1245
A collection of ashtrays
Six ashtrays. One inscribed Pernod, green glass. One from Locanda Cipriani. One inscribed Roma. One amber cut glass. One blue blown glass. One from St. John Restaurant, London. Sizes vary.
$20–40   (6)
Included in lot are two packs of American Spirits and one pack of Marlboro Lights, containing varying numbers of cigarettes, which were hidden by Doolan in various places around Celadon House. On a piece of paper rolled up inside one of the packs is a note in Doolan's script that reads: *"If you are reading this you must have wanted one pretty bad."*

LOT 1246
A backgammon set
A leather backgammon game set. One outside case corner is slightly charred; otherwise good condition.
16 x 10¾ x 2½ in.
$50–75

LOT 1247
A handwritten note
A double-sided handwritten note from Morris to Doolan. Reads in part: *"I want this to work, but there are sides to you I just can't handle sometimes. When you raise your voice and throw things, I shut down and go cold. I know this makes it worse, but I can't help it. Chucking the backgammon board into the fire was the last straw . . ."* On reverse is a handwritten note from Doolan to Morris. Reads in part: *"There are some things I need to feel loved and secure. There are some things I need to build trust, to feel safe. One of those things is being able to talk through disagreements and have the feeling that we want to come out the other end together, not that one of us has to prove the other person wrong . . ."* 11 x 8½ in.
$10–20

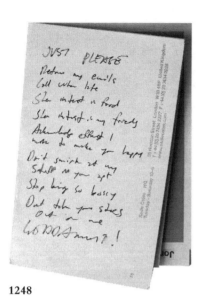

1248

1249

LOT 1248
A handwritten note

A list on the back of a gallery invitation, in Doolan's script: *"JUST PLEASE / Return my e-mails / Call when late / Show interest in food / Show interest in my friends / Acknowledge efforts I make to make you happy / Don't smirk at my stuff in your apt / Stop being so bossy / Don't take your stress out on me / GoDDAmmit!"* 7 x 6 in.
$10–20

LOT 1249
An agenda

A Smythson of Bond Street Day-to-a-page Diary, 2005. Entry for August 13 reads: *"Pick up drycleaning / Dr. Zilkha 230 / paper for Ann / tea / lg coffee / corn muffin / iced latte / carrot sticks / replace stock pot / I think I hate Hal."* 5½ x 7½ x ¾ in.
$15–25

LOT 1250
Country Life magazine

A copy of *Country Life* magazine, August 18, 2005. Laid in is a boarding pass from Virgin Atlantic Airlines; note inside in Morris's script reads: *"Bananas / loo paper / Criterion / Jason MPRC / Replace stock pot."*
$15–25

1250

1251

1252

1253

LOT 1251

A photograph

A color print of Harold Morris and Lenore Doolan. 6 x 4 in. Taken by Jason Fank.

$20–30

Doolan kept this photo in her desk at *The New York Times.*

LOT 1252

A photograph

A black-and-white photograph of Lenore Doolan. Taken by Morris. Some wear to edges. 7 x 5 in.

$20–30

Morris kept this photo in the sun visor of his car.

LOT 1253

An unusual chair and a handwritten note

A vintage 1930s leather and oak chair. Good condition, some marking to leather. A note on the back of a receipt for groceries reads: *"You said you'd be back at 8, you could have called. Have gone to the movies. Here's your present—Happy Birthday. L 9:45."* 24 in. wide x 30 in. high x 18 in. deep.

$700–900

LOT 1254

A handwritten letter

A handwritten letter from Ann Doolan to Lenore Doolan, dated March 19, 2005. Reads in part: *"It seems particularly hard for Hal to know when he hurts your feelings, etc. It's about whether you can deal with something that seems like it's maybe never going to change—is it worth it. How much pain does it cause you basically. Life seems like a matter of weighing pain versus pleasure and saying well there's enough pleasure for me to stay with this person and when there isn't enough anymore you get out. No one's going to be perfect, the problem is it's really really hard to get out of things. I recently reread a diary from when I was with Stephen and couldn't believe how unhappy I obviously was but wasn't aware of being because the momentum is always to stay in it. It's scary and lonely to get out of it, even if you're pretty sure there's a way that you'll be happier. That amount of pain prevents us from cutting the ties. You know my relationship with Stephen was about 8 and ½ years too long, and I'm not even kidding . . ."* Pale green Kate Spade laid notepaper. 8 x 5¾ in. *Not illustrated.*

$10–15

1255

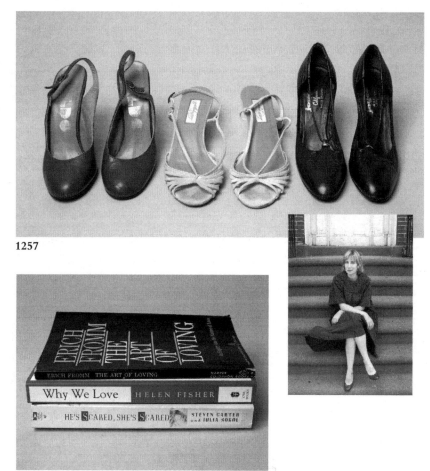

1257

1258

LOT 1255
A group of business cards
Business cards collected by the couple, including Scissors Palace, Mildred's Vegetarian Restaurant, Seventh Village Cleaners, Biography Bookshop, Quest Diagnostics, and Vino Enoteca, on back of which is written: "Couples therapist 212 555 7281." All 2½ x 3 in.
$5–10   (14)

LOT 1256
A newspaper clipping
A clipping of Doolan's *Cakewalk* column, dated September 13, 2005, on oven bottom cake. Title: "A Cake of Bits and Pieces." 8¾ x 2½ in.
Not illustrated.
$5–10

LOT 1257
Three pairs of women's shoes
Three pairs of shoes. One pair of brown round-toe sling-back heels, label inside reading "Aldo." One pair of white suede sandals, label inside reading "Rachel Comey." One pair of dark blue heels, label inside reading "Joyce California."
$50–60   (3)
Included is a photograph of Doolan on the stairs of 11A Sherman Street, wearing the brown sling-backs and the coat mentioned in Lot 1242. 6 x 4 in.

LOT 1258
Self-help and relationship books
The Art of Loving by Erich Fromm (Harper & Row, 1962); *Why We Love* by Dr. Helen Fisher (Henry Holt and Co., 2004); *He's Scared, She's Scared* by Steven Carter and Julia Sokol (Dell Trade Paperback,1995).
$20–30   (3)

LOT 1259

An invitation

An invitation to the Subramanian-Vitale Halloween party 2005. 5 x 7 in.

$5–10

1259

LOT 1260

A group of three photographs

One photograph of the couple in Halloween costume, Doolan dressed as Annie Hall, Morris as Woody Allen. One photograph of Morris as Woody Allen talking to an unknown woman in Hawaiian costume. One photograph of Doolan as Annie Hall with Hugh Nash. 4 x 6 in.

$10–20   (3)

LOT 1261

A printout of an e-mail containing address information

An e-mail from Morris to Doolan. Reads in full: *From: hmorris256@yahoo.com*

To: lenore_doolan@nytimes.com

Date: November 15, 2005

Subject: Hi

Iceland is gorgeous, but the job is dull. I'm at Hôtel Borg, Posthusstraeti 11, 101 Reykjavik, ph 551 1440, fax 551 1420. I know things must have been difficult for you this past week. I am sorry for the pain I've caused due to the uncertainty of it all. But the time apart has been good. I'm still uncertain about what I need, and need to address how unhappy I've been, but truly I do want things to work, please know that. I'll see you at Marianne's for Thanksgiving? Let's talk then.

11 x 8½ in.

Not illustrated.

$10–15

1260

LOT 1262

Gourmet **magazine**

The November 2005 issue of *Gourmet*. Laid in is an unsent letter from Doolan to Morris, dated November 14, 2005. Letter reads in part: *"Last night I picked up the film we shot from the last weekend we spent at home. I lay on the bed looking through the prints. There were these ones I'd shot of you at the table, reading the paper and drinking tea. I felt warmth and panic and huge jolting strangeness and missing. I want so much for you to be happy, for you to know what you want. There is this hope I have in us that is strong but complicated . . . don't throw us away yet."* On yellow foolscap paper. 11 x 8½ in.

$8–12

1262

1264

1263

LOT 1263
A group of photographs
One group photograph from the Grau–Melnychuk
Thanksgiving. Left to right: Lenore Doolan, Marianne
Grau, Harold Morris, Peter Melnychuk, Suzanne
Melnychuk. One photograph of Grau, Doolan, and
Morris. Four photographs of the group playing charades.
One photograph of Doolan with Peter Melnychuk's dog,
Harriet. 4 x 6 in.

$15–25   (7)

LOT 1264
A plastic shark
A plastic shark belonging to Morris. Snout has been
chewed off. 2 x 11⅛ in.
$5–10

Doolan began dogsitting Harriet for Peter Melnychuk and Marianne Grau.

LOT 1265
A newspaper clipping
A clipping of Doolan's *Cakewalk* column, dated November
29, 2005, on Truman Capote's Christmas memory
fruitcake. Title: "A Cake for Your Dearest and Nearest."
Column begins: *"Imagine a morning in late November . . ."*
8 x 2½ in.
Not illustrated.
$5–10

1266

LOT 1266
Set of ornaments
Three Mexican tin Christmas tree ornaments of the Three Wise Men. Given to the couple by Doolan's parents. Good condition. 5¼ in. in height.
$15–20   (3)

1267

LOT 1267
A candle with a handmade label
A candle with label reading *"Bougie Pour Nos Amis, Gold, Frankincense, Myrrh, Happy Holidays from Lenore and Hal"* leftover from candles given by the couple as Christmas gifts. 3¼ in. in height.
$55–75

1268

LOT 1268
Homemade pom-poms
Pom-poms made by Doolan for tree decorations. Dimensions vary.
$10–15   (12)

1269

LOT 1269

A teapot

A dog teapot marked "Made in Scotland" (chips and losses). Height 7 in.

$12–20

1270

LOT 1270
A quilt
An antique patchwork quilt, given by Doolan to Morris. Some
wear, some holes and fading. 76 x 52 in.

$100–140

Included is a photograph of the bedroom at Celadon House, where the quilt can be
seen in situ.

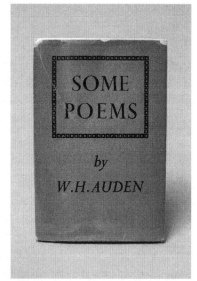

1272

1271

1273

LOT 1271

A collection of art

A framed black-and-white photograph by Stéphane Sednaoui of his then-girlfriend, Björk. Purchased by Morris as a gift for Doolan. 24 x 18 in. A framed plate of "Yoko Standing" from the book *Yoko* by Don Brown. 6½ x 8¾ in. A framed postcard of Edward Weston's "Nude, 1936." 7 x 9 in.

$200–300 (3)

LOT 1272

Auden, W. H.

Some Poems, first edition (Faber and Faber, 1937). Used, some wear. Inscription reads: *"Some X's for H . . ."*

$40–55

LOT 1273

Woolf, Virginia

A Haunted House and Other Stories (Hogarth Press, 1950), first edition. Good condition, some markings on pages. Inscription on flyleaf reads: *"For L, love H, Xmas 2005."*

$40–55

1274

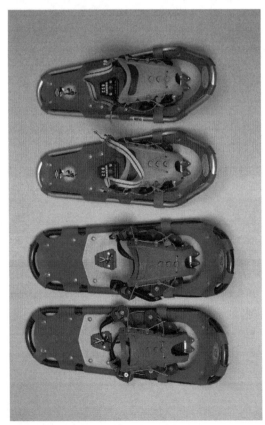

1275

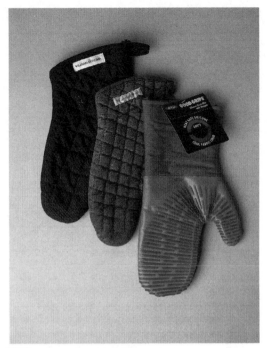

1276

LOT 1274
A collection of oven mitts
Doolan's collection of oven mitts: one from Williams Sonoma, one vintage Conran, and one Isi silicon. The silicon one is new with tag. Others well worn.
$20–45   (3)

LOT 1275
Snowshoes
Two pairs of Atlas snowshoes, one men's, one women's. Lightly worn. Sizes men's 11, women's 9.
$100–150   (2)

LOT 1276
A mix CD
A homemade mix CD made by Morris for Doolan titled *"Merry Melodies for Lally from Hally."* Image on cover is a detail from an Alfred Franck oil painting. Song list: *"Christmas Song,"* The Raveonettes / *"I'll Be Home for Christmas,"* Aimee Mann / *"God Rest Ye Merry Gentlemen,"* Bright Eyes / *("Just Like Christmas"),* Low / *"Christmas Party (featuring Nicole Sheahan),"* The Walkmen / *"Silent Night,"* Klaus Nomi / *"I Saw Three Ships,"* Sufjan Stevens / *"Christmas at the Zoo,"* The Flaming Lips / *"Frosty the Snowman,"* Cocteau Twins / *"I'm Gonna Lasso Santa Claus,"* Brenda Lee / *"It's Christmas Time,"* Yo La Tengo / *"The Christmas Waltz,"* Peggy Lee / *"We Three Kings,"* Sufjan Stevens / *"Blue Christmas,"* Low / *"Gloria in Excelsis,"* Pond. 4¾ x 5½
$20–35

LOT 1277

A note on a takeout flyer

A handwritten note in Doolan's script on the back of takeout flyer. Reads: *"H — AM LOCKED OUT! 9PM I CAN HEAR YOUR CELL INSIDE! FREEZING! I'LL BE AT STARBUCKS / 10PM. STILL LOCKED OUT. WHERE ARE YOU? WILL BE AT MALACY'S / 1AM— STILL LOCKED OUT. AT BAR. COME GET ME."* 10 x 4 in.
$10–15

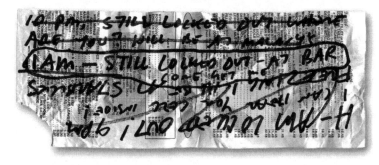

1277

LOT 1278

Two wedding placecards

Wedding placecards, one inscribed "Lenore Doolan," the other "Harold Morris," from the wedding of Adam Bainbridge and Luba Polarski, January 13, 2006. On reverse of Morris's card is the following exchange, alternating between Morris and Doolan: *"Who is this? / Stepbrother / Are you moved? / Yes! / You love weddings / They move me! / I thought you not-marrying type / I'd like someone to love me enough to want to marry me / I love you / Thanks."* 5 x 3 in.
$10–20   (2)

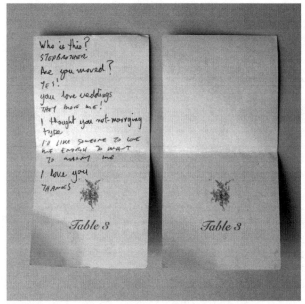

1278

LOT 1279

Three spice jars full of quarters

Jars in cylindrical form. Labels read "Spanish Saffron," "Cinnamon Sticks," "Poppy Seed." Kept for tolls and parking meters in the glove compartment of Morris's Honda. Dimensions vary.
$35–75   (3)

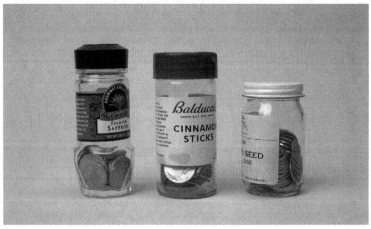

1279

LOT 1280

A series of photographs of the couple

A series of five black-and-white photographs, taken by Doolan. Doolan cast herself and Morris in the roles of Ted Hughes and Sylvia Plath, Ernest Hemingway and Martha Gelhorn, Richard and Linda Thompson, Woody Allen and Diane Keaton, and the couple in the Duane Michals photograph "This Photograph Is My Proof." All 3¼ x 4¼ in.

$25–50 (5)

1281

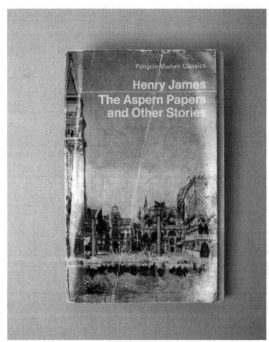

1282

LOT 1281
Salt and pepper shakers

Six pairs of salt and pepper shakers stolen by the couple from various restaurants. Sizes vary.
$30–35   (6)

LOT 1282
James, Henry

The Aspern Papers and Other Stories (Penguin Modern Classics, 1976), paperback copy. Some wear. Written in ballpoint pen on page 89 in Morris's hand are the lyrics to the song "One of These Things First" by Nick Drake. Reads in part: *"I would be / I should be so near."*
7⅛ x 4½ x ¼ in.
$10–20

1283

LOT 1283

A group of T-shirts

Eighteen T-shirts belonging to Harold Morris, acquired between 2003 and 2006. One St. Paul's Crusaders team T-shirt, label reading "Mason." One dark blue polo shirt, label reading "Chemise Lacoste." One Boston T-shirt, label reading "Perrin Pro-Weight." One Colts T-shirt, label reading "Jerzees Heavyweight Blend." One Battles T-shirt, no label. One University of Toronto T-shirt, no label. One Dodgers T-shirt, no label. One khaki T-shirt, label reading "Helmut Lang." One gray-and-white polo shirt, label reading "An Original Penguin by Munshingwear." One brown T-shirt, label reading "Helmut Lang." One black Jay Jay's Lounge T-shirt, no

label. One Vogue T-shirt, label reading "Russel Athletics." One gray T-shirt, label reading "James Perse." One black T-shirt with outer-space theme, label reading "Emerson Cotton." One Glenville 59–60, 65–68, '70, '73, '74, '75 T-shirt, label reading "Supertee." One I'm Proud to Be a Filipino T-shirt, label reading "Belton Preshrunk." One black Marshall T-shirt, label illegible. One Baxter Fishing Equipment T-shirt, label reading "Screen Stars." $100–125

(18)

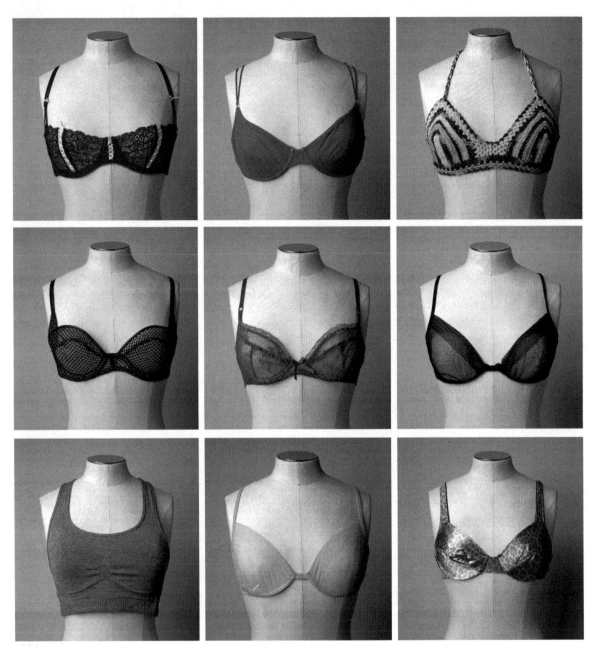

1284

LOT 1284
A group of bras

Eighteen bras belonging to Lenore Doolan, acquired between 2003 and 2006. One black-and-yellow lace, label reading "Carol Malony." One red double-strap nylon, label reading "Cosabella." One multicolored crocheted bra, no label. One pink-and-black check, label reading "Agent Provocateur." One pink nylon, label reading "Cosabella." One black nylon, label reading "Cosabella." One gray nylon and spandex sports bra, label reading "Champion." One brown with tan piping, label reading "Eres." One leopard-print nylon, label reading "Vassarette." One red-

and-white heart motif, no label. One brown ruched, label reading "Chantal Thomass." One black-and-tartan nylon, label reading "Burberry." One yellow lace, label reading "Elle MacPherson Intimates." One white-and-navy cotton with buttons, label reading "Lovable." One black-and-tan nylon, label reading "Myla." One black cotton and spandex, label reading "Calvin Klein." One black lace, label reading "Huit." One cream silk, label reading "Vivienne Corset Shoppe."

$100–170

(18)

1288

LOT 1285

A letter from *The Washington Post*

A letter for Doolan from the Arts and Life desk at *The Washington Post*, offering her a full-time job as a food section writer and secondary restaurant critic.

Not illustrated.

$10–15

LOT 1286

A handwritten letter

A letter from Morris to Doolan, on Swisshotel Zurich letterhead, dated January 29, 2006. Reads in part: *"It means a great deal to me that you won't go. I selfishly think it is the right decision, and know it makes sense for the two of us . . ."*

Not illustrated.

$10–15

LOT 1287

Handwritten drafts of a letter

Drafts of a letter to *The Washington Post* Arts and Life desk editor, declining the offer, in longhand on yellow foolscap. 11 x 8½ in.

Not illustrated.

$5–10

LOT 1288

A scrapbook

A scrapbook of pages torn from shelter magazines, wallpaper, fabric, and paint chip samples. 12 x 9 in.

$20–45

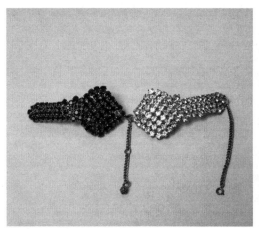

1290

1291

LOT 1289
A newspaper clipping

A clipping of Doolan's *Cakewalk* column, dated
February 3, 2006, on lemon drizzle cake. Title:
"Brighten the Corners." Column begins: *"Puckering
is a funny reflex, you pucker for a kiss, from being
waterlogged, from a tart sharp taste . . ."* 7¾ x 2½ in.
Not illustrated.

$5–10

LOT 1290
A bracelet

A bracelet given by Morris to Doolan of two keys
rendered in rhinestones. 6 in. in length.

$12–15

LOT 1291
A Valentine's Day card

A Valentine from Doolan to Morris. Reads in full:
"I still love you."

$12–15

LOT 1292
A menu

A Valentine's Day menu, hand-drawn by Doolan:
*"American Caviar on Iceberg / Heart-shaped Radishes /
Pink Turtle Soup / Foie Gras Morris / Wrapped Squab
& Sauce / Grapefruit Maraschino / Doolan-Decker Red
Velvet Cake / Coffee and Charbonnel Chocolates / Wine:
Le Cigar Volant, Bonny Doon, 1994."* 6¾ x 4½ in.

$50–65

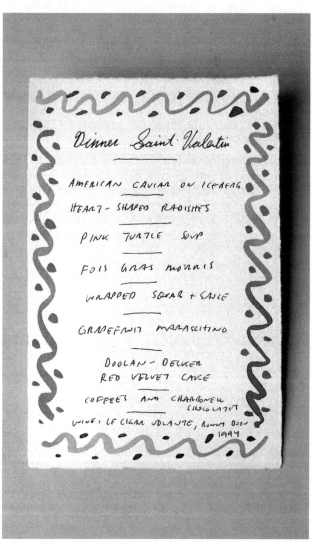

1292

115

1293

1294

1295

LOT 1293
Paint

A set of eight Farrow and Ball sample pots of paint in "Shaded White," "Dead Salmon," "Folly Green," "Arsenic," "Pigeon," "Matchstick," "Down Pipe," and "Savage Ground."

$10–30   (8)

LOT 1294
A theater playbill for *Abigail's Party*

A playbill from *Abigail's Party*. Handwriting in margins alternates between Doolan and Morris: *"Why go through my e-mail? / His message was creepy. / You should trust me. / I ~~don't~~ can't trust you. / I can't handle your suspicion."* 8½ x 5¼ in.

$10–15

LOT 1295
A Gotland sheepskin rug

A dark Gotland sheepskin rug. Purchased by Morris in Copenhagen, March 2006. Good condition.

$40–55

Rug was installed on Morris's side of the bed.

1296

1297

LOT 1296
A group of paintings
Five thrift-store paintings collected by the couple.
Dimensions vary.
$20–45   (5)

LOT 1297
An invitation
An invitation from Doolan and Morris for a "(Renovations
to our House) Warming Party," May 2006. 5⅜ x 4½ in.
$10–15

LOT 1298
A color-changing lamp
A Mathmos pulse lamp. Given to the couple by Jason Frank.
7½ x 4¼ x 2½ in.
Not illustrated.
$50–60

1299

LOT 1299
A group of knitted food
Knitted cauliflower, oreo, beet, brussels sprout, battenburg cake, cucumber, hot cross bun, two cupcakes, bean, mushroom, doughnut, and cherries. Given to the couple by Kyle Kaplan.
$15–20   (13)

LOT 1300
Paper bookmark from St. Mark's Bookshop
On verso, in Doolan's hand, is written: *"Walter / Lucas / Matthew / Pierre / Vera / Zelda / Cloghda / Bronwyn."* 7 x 1¾
Not illustrated.
$5–10

LOT 1301
A newspaper clipping
A clipping of Doolan's *Cakewalk* column, dated May 29, 2006, on bara brith. Title: "Black Tea, Spice, and Everything Nice." 7⅛ x 2½ in.
Not illustrated.
$5–10

LOT 1302
A group of yard sale finds
A vintage hand-knit green wool zippered sweater, child size, ca. 1940. A rainbow necklace. A VHS copy of *Annie Hall*. An oversize plastic die. A heart-shaped brooch. Dimensions vary.
$40–80   (5)

1302

1303

LOT 1303

A stuffed squirrel

A stuffed gray squirrel, found in an antique shop.

8⅜ in. in height.

$50–75

Included are two photographs, one of Doolan with the squirrel, pretending to feed it, and the other of Morris playing Scrabble with the squirrel.

LOT 1304

Agenda

Smythson of Bond St. Day-to-a-page Diary for 2006. Entry for June 11 reads: *"12 late / preg poss. / Pros: / not avoiding life / baby / family unit / create a real home / get on with it / feel a part of the world. Cons: scared of spending rest of life with H / Hal not around / won't get married / H's friends all regret having children / don't want to feel so much doubt about this / don't know if I want Hal's baby."*

Not illustrated.

$15–25

1305

LOT 1305
Moore, Pamela

Chocolates for Breakfast (Longman's Green and Co., 1957).

Laid in is a double-sided handwritten note from Doolan to Morris on a page torn from a reporter's notebook. Reads: *"Hal, am out for a walk. I think I might be pregnant. Please call me when you get this, I bought a pee test but want to discuss how we feel before I take it. Love, L."* On reverse of note is written in Morris's script: *"Darling one, sorry to leave just a note in reply, but please understand I need some time to think too. Was not even going to stop home but forgot hard drive—am dashing en-route to Vermont to re-shoot for the next three days. Will call you from the hotel. I'm sorry, I know this seems bad but I need some space to think, please understand. Take the test, we'll figure it out— It'll all be good. H x."*
$12–20

1306

LOT 1306

A white noise machine

A No. 500 Sleep Sound by Invento white noise machine, kept by Morris in the bedroom of 11a Sherman Street. Irreparable damage to top and sides, as if struck by a hammer.
$5–12

LOT 1307

An Hermès wristwatch

An Hermès Arceau women's wristwatch with blue calfskin watchband. Some wear to band, otherwise good condition. Included is original box.
$500–900

Included is a handwritten note from Morris to Doolan reading: *"I did not handle that at all well, and the circumstances were terrible. This is for you, and in apology, and though it wasn't meant to be this time, perhaps next? Love, Hal."*

1307

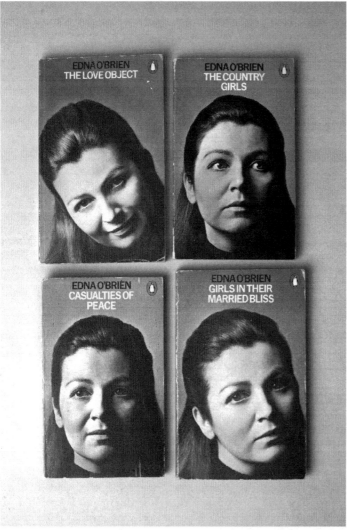

1308

1309

1310

LOT 1308

O'Brien, Edna

Four paperback books: *The Love Object, The Country Girls, Girls in Their Married Bliss,* and *Casualties of Peace* (Penguin, 1967–70), all inscribed "Lenore Doolan" in upper right on flyleaf.

$50–65 (4)

LOT 1309

A group of paperback books

Seven Harold Pinter and Tom Stoppard books, all inscribed "Harold Morris" in upper right on flyleaf. *The Caretaker* by Harold Pinter (Eyre Methuthen, 1974); *Dirty Linen* by Tom Stoppard (Faber, 1976); *The Real Inspector Hound* by Tom Stoppard (Grove Press, 1975); *The Birthday Party* by Harold Pinter (Grove Press, 1981); *Three Plays* by Harold Pinter (Grove Press, 1962); *Jumpers* by Tom Stoppard (Grove Press, 1972); *Arcadia* by Tom Stoppard (Faber and Faber, 1988).

$50–65 (7)

LOT 1310

A postcard

A postcard from Jaipur, India; from Morris to Doolan. Note on verso reads: *"India-digestion, but otherwise great. Might stay on longer. X H."* 4 x 6 in.

$10–15

1313

1314

LOT 1311
A printout of an e-mail containing address information
A printout of an e-mail from Morris in India to Doolan in New York, dated June 6, 2006. Reads: *From: hmorris256@yahoo.com*
To: lenore_doolan@nytimes.com
Date: June 6, 2006
Subject: HEY
Been thinking—you'll be busy working late due to the promotion, so think I'm going to stay on longer and travel for the next 2 months with Ben. I've been needing a break like this.
11 x 8½ in.
Not illustrated.
$10–15

LOT 1312
A phone bill
A phone bill from the Hotel Bangalore Gate, totaling $800. 11 x 8½ in.
Not illustrated.
$5–10

LOT 1313
A birthday card
A birthday card from Morris in India to Doolan. Reads in part: *"Am sorry to be missing your birthday, Lenore. I think we are on the same page with this, I think we both need time and space to think things over . . ."* Some creases, as card has been folded in half. 7½ x 6 in.
$15–20

LOT 1314
A group of photographs
Photographs of summer dinner parties given at Celadon, which Doolan rented with friends Adam Bainbridge and Luba Polarski. 4 x 6 in.
$10–20   (10)

1315

LOT 1315

A group of vintage dresses

One brown-and-blue-flowers print dress, no label. One rust geometrical-pattern tea dress, label reading "Lanvin." One print dress, label reading "Chix Hawaii Liberty House." One green-and-pink floral pattern 1960s-era dress, label cut out.

$50–60

(4)

1318

1316

LOT 1316
A recipe binder
Celadon House recipe binder, kept by Doolan for three summers. 12 x 9 in.
$10–20

LOT 1317
A clutch purse
A vintage Victorian clutch purse, black grosgrain ribbon exterior and silk interior. Good condition. Enclosed in interior pocket is an invitation to a book party for Adam Bainbridge at *The Paris Review*. On verso is written: *"Erich: eril025@yahoo.com."*
Not illustrated.
$20–45
The party took place on the night of Morris's return from India. Morris was not in attendance.

LOT 1318
Sagan, Françoise
Four paperback novels: *Scars on the Soul* (Penguin, 1977); *Aimez-vous Brahms* (Penguin, 1960); *Sunlight on Cold Water* (Penguin, 1971); *La Chamade* (Penguin, 1971). In *La Chamade* is the underlined passage: *"There can never be enough said of the virtues, the dangers, the powers of a shared laugh."*
$10–15   (4)

LOT 1319

A studio photograph

A photograph of Morris, taken in a New Delhi portrait photographer's studio. 10 x 8 in.

$10–20

LOT 1320

Receipt from restaurant

A receipt from Wallse restaurant, dated August 29, 2006, reading: *"4 Gruner Vertliner, 1 Gin Martini, 1 Whitefish app, 1 beetroot app, 4 lake trout, 1 schnitzel."* (Last two items canceled.) 5 x 3⅜ in.

Not illustrated.

$5–15

LOT 1321

A handwritten letter

A handwritten letter from Ann Doolan to Lenore Doolan. Reads in part: *"Well, fighting feels bad for everyone. The key is to be realistic about how often and how low the lows are. It doesn't have to be always sturm and drang. I used to always talk about how I pitied the boring couples who never experienced any of our highs and lows, but I decided it's hard to get things done with the highs and lows. You spend a lot of time avoiding life. Stephen was a long excuse to avoid life for me, and I have to admit I can see some of that with you and Hal. It has nothing to do with happy. For me it was about joining life and being sort of normal and happier in a different way. Len, it's gonna be hard, but I think it's good you're taking a break. You got used to him being away this summer anyway! Do you want me to come stay with you for a few weeks? I could research from there . . ."*

Not illustrated.

$10–20

LOT 1322

A photograph and a costume sketch

A photograph of Lenore and Ann Doolan at 11A Sherman Street. A sketch by Lenore Doolan of Halloween costume plans for the sisters. Lenore Doolan as a litmus test, Ann Doolan as marshmallow. 11 x 8.5 in.

$10–15   (2)

LOT 1323

A newspaper clipping

A clipping of Doolan's *Cakewalk* column, dated November 29, 2006, on Paris-Brest. Title: "The Sweetest Thing." 9 x 2½ in.

Not illustrated.

$5–10

1319

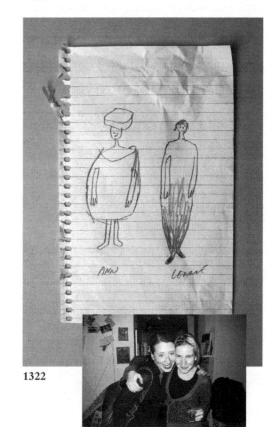

1322

1325

LOT 1324
Beard, Jo Ann

The Boys of My Youth (Little, Brown, 1998), hardcover, first
edition. Some wear to jacket and pages. A handwritten list in
the margins of page 147 reads: *"Goodwill / Dr. Zilkha 430 / Tea
/ Canteloupe / shrimp wrap / latte / carrot sticks / cancel w/Erich / 8
sherrys headache/ Erich / presumptuous."*
Not illustrated.
$12–15

LOT 1325
***Gourmet* reading supplement**

A copy of a *Gourmet* supplement, Fall 2006. Laid in is a
handwritten letter from Morris to Doolan. Reads in part: *"Your
ideas about friendship are beautiful and I can only hope we can get to
that. I'm in the midst of figuring out what I need these days. I'm glad
to hear you want to try to be my friend."*
$10–20

LOT 1326
James, William

Pragmatism: A New Name for Some Old Ways of Thinking, paperback
edition, 1907 (Hackett Publishing Company, 1980). Laid in is a
handwritten letter from Doolan to Morris. Reads in part: *"The
sound of your voice stirs up a volcano of emotion I'm trying very hard to
control. Please respect my silence. You remain extremely special to me,
but let's keep our distance . . ."*
$10–20

1326

1327

1329

1330

LOT 1327
Four stuffed animals
Three bears and one elephant. Various sizes.
$150–195   (4)

LOT 1328
Real estate listings
Real estate listings for one-bedroom apartments
in Manhattan; options circled in Sharpie. Real
estate listings for one-bedroom apartments in
Los Angeles; options circled in pencil.
Dimensions vary.
Not illustrated.
$5–10

LOT 1329
A dog's head eggcup
One porcelain dog's head eggcup. Made in
Germany. 2¾ x 2¼ in.
$10–12

LOT 1330
Corks
Champagne and wine corks from various
occasions. Dates ranging between 1989 and 2006.
$10–12   (9)

1331

LOT 1331

A group of dried flower petals

A group of dried flower petals from various occasions, kept and pressed by Morris.

$20–45   (7)

1332

LOT 1332
A group of dried and pressed four-leaf clovers
A group of four-leaf clovers from various places, kept and pressed by Doolan.
$20–45   (6)

For Adam Penn Gilders

Acknowledgments

Thank you, Sheila Heti and Paul Sahre—Sheila, especially, for helping me understand what this book is about. Thank you to Jason Fulford for hours of picture-taking and thoughtful advice; to Michael Schmelling, Derek Shapton, and Kristen Sjaarda for their excellent photographs; to Deirdre Dolan for her encouragement and enthusiasm; to Craig Taylor for music and major themes; and to Sara Angel, Pamela Baguley, Rachel Comey, Hernan Diaz, Joy Goodwin, Cailey Hall, Jessica Johnson, Abby Kagan, Rita Konig, Jason Logan, Paul Marlow, Rebecca Nagel, Emily Oberman, Laura Peterson, Gus Powell, Miranda Purves, Mary Robertson, Anne Ross, Tim Rostron, Gwen Smith, Dianna Symonds, Kim Temple, Elaine Whitmire, Ken Whyte, Jere Wile, and Margaux Williamson for help, notes, and stories. Thanks to Andrew Wylie for his invaluable insight, and to Sarah Crichton for her unfailing support and trust.

I am grateful to my cast of friends who rallied over potato chips, coffee, cake, and wine. Special thanks to Bob and Lorna, who don't throw anything away. And to James Truman, with love. (Also to BC, NB, and PG, whose artifacts remain important.)

Leanne Shapton is an illustrator, writer and publisher who was born in Toronto and now lives in New York. She is the art director of the *New York Times* op-ed page and cofounder of J&L Books, a nonprofit publishing company specializing in new photography, art and fiction. She is the author of *Was She Pretty?*.